MONSTER SQUAD
THE SLIME THAT WOULD NOT DIE

title tyler

BY LAURA DOWER
ILLUSTRATED BY DAVE SCHLAFMAN

SCHOLASTIC INC.
New York Toronto London Auckland
Sydney Mexico City New Delhi Hong Kong

ISBN-13: 978-0-545-21143-7
ISBN-10: 0-545-21143-3

12 11 10 9 8 7 6 5 4 3 2 1   9 10 11 12 13 14/0

Printed in the U.S.A.   40

First Scholastic printing, September 2009

For Papa.

With special thanks to Forrest Ackerman,
aka Forry, the king of B-Monster movies; master
of the monster pun; and real-life inspiration for
Oswald Leery.

—Laura Dower

To Genna . . . who said I always could do this.
—Dave Schlafman

TABLE OF CONTENTS

Prologue: Jesse Ranger.. 6

Chapter 1: Bigger Than Rodiak............................... 11

Chapter 2: What's a Dork Like Me Doing in VIP?...19

Chapter 3: There's No Escaping from the Goo,
Especially Not for You..................................... 29

Chapter 4: One *Bluuurp* Beyond........................... 36

Chapter 5: The Great Flood...................................... 42

Chapter 6: My Teacher Is Missing!......................... 47

Chapter 7: The Ninja Knows................................... 59

Chapter 8: On Top of Nerve Mountain 67

Chapter 9: Danger Man.. 77

Chapter 10: Doctor Leery, I Presume?................. 85

Chapter 11: Smells Like Feet.................................. 93

Chapter 12: Do Not Touch . . . Or Else.............. 101

Chapter 13: Curses! Slimo Again!....................... 109

Chapter 14: Welcome to Moldy City.................... 115

Chapter 15: *Thwunk*... 123

Chapter 16: A Sizzle in the Air............................ 134

JESSE RANGER

There are a zillion things that make my hometown of Riddle weird. Like Tricks, the three-legged dog that hangs outside the library and growls at you if you have overdue books. Or the three gigantic windmills that just appeared one day out on Route 5. Or stores at Petroglyph Mall that everyone swears are haunted. But nothing in Riddle rates higher on the weird-o-meter than Leery Castle. It sits at the top of Nerve Mountain, all creepy and quiet, like it's watching me.

I'm beginning to think that maybe it is.

Leery Castle was built in the early 1900s. The first Leery to live there was Lucas Leery. He made silent movies. Then there was Desmond Leery, Lucas Leery's son. He was born in 1910 and made movies with his father. Together they made some of the most well-known movies of the time: dramas, romances, thrillers, and comedies. They created a new filming technique with a special camera no one had ever seen before. It made everything pop off the screen, almost like 3-D vision, but without funny glasses. People loved it.

Then Oswald Leery came along. He's Lucas Leery's grandson. When he inherited the family movie business, Oswald Leery decided to make only one kind of movie: the monster movie. But his movie monsters weren't your typical Frankenstein or Wolf Man. Leery's monsters had crooked fangs, laser-beam eyes, and fake blood like ketchup. You could actually see on-screen where fur was glued on. They had funny names like Rodiak and Chomp-O.

Critics made fun of Leery's movies. They called his creatures B-Monsters. But Leery didn't mind the name. He loved it so much that he renamed the special Leery family filming process B-Monster Vision. It made even the most fake-looking monsters come alive on-screen. With B-Monster Vision, flying bats seemed to fly for *real*, off the screen and right into my face.

Tuesday is the one night each week that Mom works late at the art gallery, so Dad and I always watch movies together during dinner. It was on a rainy Tuesday night last year when Dad showed me my first-ever Oswald Leery B-Monster double feature: *Bog Beast* and *Island of Dr. Dim.*

I will never forget the exact moment when the Bog Beast jumps out of the swamp and swallows this mutant crocodile in one gulp. I snorted chocolate milk out of my nose—I was *that* scared. But I couldn't look away. Those special effects were so bad, they were great.

I've been hooked on Bs ever since.

All in all, Leery made sixty-three B-Monster movies, including sequels. I wish he had made even more. But seventeen years ago, he stopped making Bs—just like that.

Dad says that one day Leery disappeared into his castle and never came out again.

Most people in Riddle say that Leery went bonkers. But I don't think that's possible. The guy was a genius—not nuts. I should know: My Great Uncle Rich was a stuntman for B-Monsters once. He and Leery were best buds.

Other people think maybe Leery got a bad case of agoraphobia. That means he got so afraid of public places that he couldn't leave his castle anymore. But he's not agora-*anything*. He always loved his fans. Oswald Leery used to give guided tours of his castle to show off his huge collection of B-Monster stuff. Dad told me Great Uncle Rich took him inside the castle a few times when Dad was a kid.

Here's what I think.

I think maybe Leery got spooked by one of his own monsters. Just the smell of Slimo is supposed to be enough to make someone's nose fall off. Or maybe, just maybe, Leery woke up one day with a terrible case of amnesia and just forgot how to make movies.

It could happen. Riddle is the land of the weird, after all.

Since I started watching Bs, I've written Oswald Leery a letter every week. I have told him all of my favorite parts from each of his films, asked him about how all the special effects were done, and, every time, I've asked him for the real reason he's still hiding out up there in his castle.

Forty-eight letters later, no one has written back

yet. Not even a postcard. And I've been losing hope, letter by letter.

But I won't give up.

Someday, I want to make my own cool movies.

I want the best director in the whole universe to tell me everything I need to know about fake blood, warty bumps, and all the other secrets of the Bs.

I want to visit Leery Castle and see all the same things my dad saw when he was a kid.

And, if I'm *really* lucky, I want to do all these things before I get out of fifth grade.

BIGGER THAN RODIAK

"Get away from me, you . . . BUG!" a woman with red hair howled.

A horned black beetle the size of a soda can whizzed behind her. It landed next to her, and its sharp pointed pincers were open, ready to strike.

"Heeyaaaah!" the woman yelped.

She stomped on the beetle with the heel of her shoe. With one earsplitting crunch, bug guts sprayed all over the place.

"That's enough of you!" she cried, wiping beetle juice off her glasses.

Clickety click. Clickety click.

The woman spun around in the darkness. Where was that noise coming from? There was a switch here, somewhere. Where?

11

There. *Click.*

A bright yellow light flooded the room.

"Nooooo!"

She was surrounded by an army of beetles just like the one she had crushed! Wings spread out like armor! Antennae twitched!

Clickety clickety click click click . . .

"Aaaaaaaah!"

The woman screamed and scrambled onto a couch. But it was too late for escape. There were too many enormous beetles scuttling toward her across the floor, like a moving carpet.

Click.

Our kitchen television winked off.

"Dad!" I exclaimed. "It was just getting to the good part."

"You mean when the beetles crawl back out of her ears?" Dad asked, smirking.

I nodded. "My favorite scene ever."

"Let's save it," Dad said. "We can watch it together later when we eat dinner. Don't you have homework to do?"

"Did it. During recess," I replied. "Just like every Tuesday, Dad."

Dad shrugged. "I should know better. Nothing gets in the way of B-Monster nights."

"Ha, ha, ha! Nothing!" I cackled like one of the giant alien turkeys in the B-Monster classic, *Space Birds Gone Wild.*

"If only I could invent a force as magnificent as B-Monster Vision," Dad said thoughtfully. "Now *that* would be something."

I smiled. The truth was, Dad probably could invent something as cool as B-Monster Vision. His name is A. E. Ranger. The *A* and *E* stand for Albert and Einstein, just like the famous scientist. Dad is part scientist, part inventor, *and* part meteorologist, which is really just a fancy-schmancy word for weather guy. Last year he invented a cool machine, the Robo-Toaster, which grills secret codes onto sandwiches.

"Want spaghetti or macaroni and cheese tonight?" Dad asked.

"Mac," I said. "With extra cheese, *please.*" I could live on a diet of cheesy noodles, Gatorade, and Blow Pops.

Even though the TV was off now, I still had B-Monster beetles on the brain. If you're not careful, Bs can spoil your appetite for dinner.

"Put those into recycling, okay?" Dad asked, pointing to a pile of newspapers.

I grabbed the papers and threw them into a large blue recycling container under our kitchen counter. Dad takes saving the planet seriously and so do I.

As I dropped the papers into the bin, a bright orange flyer caught my eye. It had a blurry photo of an old, old man on it. I recognized the mustache, hair, and glasses immediately.

"Dad! Look!" I cried, waving it in the air. It was an insert from yesterday's local newspaper. "It's Oswald Leery!"

"Read it."

My eyes raced across the page. Oswald Leery's wrinkles were so deep in the picture that they looked like someone had drawn on his face with Magic Markers. The caption read, "Legendary Riddle film director to make last-minute appearance at local library."

That gave me prickles all over.

"Jess," Dad said patiently. "Why don't you read it *out loud*?"

Please join
DOCTOR OSWALD LEERY
Director and Collector of Scary Objects
for a just-scheduled
B-Monster Movie Screening of

Slimo

Children's Reading Room
Floor 2, Riddle Library
Tuesday, September 20, 6:30 P.M.
Kids only. Register in advance at the circulation
desk. Space limited.

"Dad!" I blurted. "This is for today! This can't be for real. Is this for real?"

Dad's eyes were as wide as mine.

"Looks real to me," Dad mumbled.

"Why do you think he's making a last-minute appearance *now*?" I asked Dad. "How could I not have heard about it? Why didn't Ms. Shenanigans tell me? She knows how much I like the B-Monsters—"

"Take a breath, Jess," Dad said. "Why don't you call and see if you can still make the screening?"

Dad was right. Quickly, I dialed the main number at the library.

Busy!

Everything inside of me wanted to scream. This was way more than just some ordinary event at the library. This was big; maybe even bigger than Rodiak, the biggest B-Monster of all time! I took a great gulp of air and tried to relax, like Dad said, but relaxing was impossible. It's not every day that your biggest dream in the world falls into your recycling basket.

I dialed again.

Still busy!

It was already 5:15 P.M.

"Dad?" I asked, tapping my foot as I hit redial over and over. "Can we get all your old issues of *B-Monster Galaxy* down from the attic so I can get them signed tonight?"

Dad laughed. "All of them? Really?" he asked. "There are at least three huge cartons. We don't have time . . ."

"What about your B-Monster trading card collection?"

"Jesse," Dad said with a sigh. "The entire collection? I doubt Mr. Leery will have time to sign any of that stuff. Why don't you try to call—"

"Shhhh!" I cried. "It's ringing. Someone's picking up the phone."

"Hello?"

"Hello!" I gasped into the receiver. "Ms. Shenanigans? This is Jesse Ranger from the fifth-grade reading club, remember me?"

"Of course, Jesse," Ms. Shenanigans said. "How can I help you?"

"I need to reserve a spot for the Oswald Leery screening. It's still tonight, right?"

"Right. But, I'm sorry, Jesse, that event is full."

"Full?"

I felt all the air hiss out of me like a popped balloon.

"Oh, wait!" Ms. Shenanigans clucked. "Your name is already on our VIP list."

"Huh?"

"Yes, it's right here. Jesse Ranger!" she cheered. "At the very top of my list."

I had no idea how my name got on that list, but I wasn't going to question it. There was no time for questions now.

"If you're coming, you'd better hurry up," Ms. Shenanigans said. "Even our VIP seats fill up fast!"

"Okay. I'll be there in a snap!"

I hung up the phone and bent down to tighten my sneaker laces.

"Dad!" I yelled. "Warm up the car! We have somewhere to go and no time to get there!"

WHAT'S A DORK LIKE ME DOING IN VIP?

I nearly tripped headfirst off our bottom porch step as we raced for the car. My shoelaces had come undone already! They always do that.

Dad grabbed me by the back of my T-shirt and heaved me up. We got into the car. Dad turned the ignition key.

Chut-chut-chut.

My eyes fell on the digital car clock. 6:02.

"We're going to be late, Dad," I gasped.

"Jesse, we'll make it," Dad said with a wide smile. He leaned on the gas pedal and we revved into the road.

I breathed a sigh of relief, like Roger Rogers, the hero from *Slimo* and other Bs. Roger always says "Ready to bust some heads!" and "Motor on, monster!" Stuff like that.

"Don't tell Mom that we missed dinner, okay?" Dad said. He handed me a plastic shopping bag with a yogurt, banana, and plastic spoon. "Eat this, will you?"

"Don't worry, Dad," I told him, putting the bag on the floor. "I'm not even that hungry."

I was still thinking about the whole VIP library list. I knew VIP stood for very important person, but what did that have to do with me? Who put me on the list? I couldn't shake the thought that something really weird was going on.

Thankfully the screening was on a Tuesday—Mom's late night at work.

If she had been here, Mom probably would have dreamed up ten reasons to keep me home, especially since everything had happened at the last minute. For starters, Mom hates to rush. For another thing, she doesn't get the whole B-Monster world, no matter how many times I try to explain it.

"I really wish I could go to see Leery with you," Dad said as he changed lanes and sped up. It was 6:12.

"Me too," I said. "I can't believe you've never seen *Slimo* on the big screen."

"Too bad you didn't have time to call Garth. You two would have had fun."

Garth Gable is my funniest friend at Riddle Elementary. We like a lot of the same things: hockey, Ring Dings, Xbox, Chinese water dragons, and bettas. I just wish that Garth loved B-Monsters as much as me. But sometimes it's hard to convince friends to like the same stuff that you do, no matter how hard you try. Whenever I try to get Garth to watch Bs with me, he always finds an excuse to go home.

We pulled into the library parking lot by 6:16, our best time ever. Dad parked behind a minivan and dropped me at the curb.

"Jesse," Dad said, "I'll come back to pick you up at eight-thirty. I don't know if I'll be able to park, so meet me right here out front."

"Bye, Dad!" I jumped out of the car, slammed the door, and waved good-bye.

What a mob! There must have been a hundred kids climbing the steps toward the library's enormous carved wooden doors. There were a few adults, too, like stray moms and dads who'd come to drop off their kids and a few other grown-ups trying to sneak in on their own. It reminded me of that terrible scene in Leery's classic, *Mega Mantis*, where everyone in town gets chased by the swarm of super flies.

One guy pushed just ahead of me in the crowd. He had on dark glasses and a black leather jacket. And he was definitely not a kid! *He* actually looked like a super fly.

But something about him seemed familiar, too. I recognized a pair of blue-green sneakers. Hey! It was my science teacher!

"Mr. Bunsen?"

The crowd rushed forward.

"Mr. Bunsen?"

I tried peering over everyone's head, but I lost sight of him.

What was Mr. Bunsen doing here?

"Hey, no pushing!" some kid barked. Then he elbowed me in the side.

The closer I got to the entryway, the more dangerous it became. Another kid slammed into my shoulder and stepped on my high-tops. Then this short kid grabbed me by the jean jacket and growled like a grizzly. Kids were taking this so seriously! I had no clue other kids loved the Bs as much as I did.

At last I got through the doors and into the

children's reading room. But where was the sign that read *VIP*?

I saw at least one person I knew, another fifth-grader. Her name is Stella Min, but everyone calls her Ninja. She has long black hair that always droops in her face. I heard she has a brown belt in karate. That's why everyone calls her Ninja. I think she saw me, too, but she quickly turned and sat down in a seat near the front of the room. It was right next to the VIP sign I was looking for!

Aha! I pounced on a blue folding chair in the VIP row.

I looked around at everyone else in the section. What made all *these* kids very important? I couldn't figure it out.

And then *he* jumped in front of my face.

Damon Molloy is the boy in my class who, just last year, duct-taped a hockey puck to some kid's stomach. One time he pounded me so hard in dodge ball that I got a bruise the size of a watermelon.

"Yo, Ranger!" Damon said, smacking me on the arm.

Damon acts scary, but he looks even scarier. His spiky blond hair always makes it seem like he just poked his finger into a supercharged socket. He wears these extra-friendly T-shirts, too. Tonight's T-shirt said: STAND BACK. I MEAN IT.

"Yo, Ranger, I saw you from across the room. What's a dork like you doing in VIP?"

I wasn't sure how to answer that.

"I'm on the list," I blurted.

"Yeah, well," Damon snarled. "*That* must be a mistake. It's not the Very Idiotic Person list."

"B-b-but . . ." I stammered. "I was here."

"Just move over," Damon barked. "I need three seats for me and my VIP friends. You can sit behind us. It's the same difference."

"No, I'm sitting here," I asserted, trying hard to sound tough on the outside even though I felt more like Jell-O on the inside.

"Sitting here with who?" Damon asked, picking his ear and flicking it at me. "Your imaginary friend club? Move!"

What was I supposed to say to *that*?

I started to stand up, ready to move, but then a girl appeared.

"Jesse?"

It was Lindsey Gomez. She's in my homeroom. When Damon saw her he got this crooked grin on his face like he was about to kick us *both* to the curb.

Thankfully, his two moronic friends yelled, "DAMON! OVER HERE!" and he ditched us to go and join them in the front row. All he wanted all along was a better VIP seat.

What a relief, I thought. I turned to Lindsey.

A sleek digital camera hung around her neck, and she had a rolled-up *B-Monster Galaxy* issue under one arm.

"You read that?" I said, pointing to the magazine. Leery's photograph was on the cover.

"At least a hundred times!" Lindsey hugged the

magazine. "I love Oswald Leery so much," she said, grinning. "Do you think he'll sign this for me?"

"Sure, he might—"

"My grandfather used to take photos for B-Monster Studios a long time ago. He took the photo on the cover of this magazine," Lindsey said.

"Wow, that's—"

"Aren't you glad the library is doing this? I brought my camera to take some photos for the school paper. Did you know that this many people watched Bs?"

I shook my head and stared at the floor.

"What's the matter?" Lindsey said. "B-Monster got your tongue?"

The lights flickered.

Ms. Shenanigans stood at full attention at a table at the front of the room. She had a microphone in hand. Her head bobbed as she tried to count us one by one. She tapped the microphone. "Can everybody hear me?"

Damon and his two obnoxious friends yelled back. "WE HEAR YOU!"

Up behind the podium, next to Ms. Shenanigans, was a large, flat object covered by a drop cloth.

What was under *there*? Was it a prop from Leery's

collection? Maybe it was something cool from a brand-new B-Monster movie? *That* would be just about the best thing that could possibly happen! If I saw a sneak preview of some cool contraption or painted model from the B-Monster master's new masterpiece, I would be the happiest kid in Riddle. No, I would be the happiest kid in the United States, in North America, on the Earth, and in the entire solar system.

"Welcome, everyone, to tonight's screening of *Slimo!*" Ms. Shenanigans spoke into the microphone. "Ready to see the movie?"

Everyone cheered.

"As you know, kids, we had a very, very special guest scheduled to be here with us tonight. He is a Riddle legend. His family has been here for generations, making movies . . ."

I bit my lip. Wait. Go back.

Did Ms. Shenanigans just say that she "had" a very special guest—as in *past tense*? I wasn't sure I'd heard correctly.

"Unfortunately," Ms. Shenanigans said, "Mr. Leery had some urgent business matters to tend to. He could not make it here tonight . . ."

The crowd sighed.

"But," Ms. Shenanigans held her hands up in the air. "I have another surprise."

Low, slow, creaking music droned out of speakers nearby. It sounded just like the music Oswald Leery always plays in the Bs, like just before some unsuspecting kid gets turned into monster soup. I didn't know what we were in for, but I knew it had to be creepy—in a good way.

The lights dimmed very low.

I saw someone step out of the shadows behind Ms. Shenanigans. He was tall and skinny and wore a long cape. Or was it a coat? I couldn't tell. I couldn't see his face either.

Slowly, the mysterious figure walked toward us with arms outstretched.

My stomach did a flip-flop.

Then the room went black.

CHAPTER 3

THERE'S NO ESCAPING FROM THE GOO, ESPECIALLY NOT FOR YOU

I've never heard so much screaming in a library.

About ten seconds passed before the lights went up again, brighter than ever.

The cape on the man wasn't a cape at all, but an old-fashioned jacket with tails. He wore a high-collared shirt and tie, too, with a shiny brass watch dangling from his pocket. The man's patent-leather shoes reflected the library's fluorescent lights so that it looked like he had lightbulbs on his feet. His black hair was slicked way back, which made the man's very large forehead seem much, *much* larger than it really was. But the weirdest part was that the guy didn't stop smiling! This made him very hard to look at without, well, smiling back.

"May I present Mr. Walter Block," Ms. Shenanigans announced. "Our special guest."

"Call me Walter," Walter Block said.

We clapped politely. He smiled a little wider.

"Thank you, but I'm not the only special one here tonight," Block said. He took the microphone, walked over to the shrouded object, and pulled off its cover.

We gasped.

Oswald Leery?

Well, it wasn't *actually* Oswald Leery. It was an oversize photographic cutout, like the ones in movie theaters. The cutout had gray-tufted hair on top, like a woodpecker's head. And he wore a dark blue suit, turtleneck shirt, and trademark black glasses. You can never see his eyes in any photographs. Leery carried a large cane with a carved, silver, two-headed

serpent for a handle. It was almost as cool as having the real Leery at the library.

"I think my grandfather took that picture of him," Lindsey said proudly.

"Wow." I was impressed.

Walter went on. "Mr. Leery wanted all of you to view this very special copy of *Slimo* tonight, on loan from a very dear friend. This version includes rarely seen outtakes and never-seen-before scenes."

Everyone let out a little "ooooh," including me and Lindsey. I'd seen the original *Slimo* five times before, but not in a special place like this.

"The first *Slimo* feature was filmed back in 1955 right in downtown Riddle, not on a soundstage," Walter went on. "You may recognize some familiar locations in the movie, like the local post office."

The lights inside the library dimmed. I clenched the tops of my knees with my hands and leaned forward. Sometimes waiting to be scared is the scariest thing of all.

Presenting an Original B-Monster Movie Production!
Filmed in B-Monster Vision!

A bright green slime dribbled from the corners of the screen. It looked like it was going to drip off the edges! Soon the slime began to ooze and gush, making wet, squishy sounds, like when I walk through mud in my sneakers. Then the slime shaped itself into five letters and a gooey exclamation point.

Slimo!

I barely even blinked for the next hour and a half, right up until the part when Slimo gets as big as a school bus and grows teeth! It devours the last person in Riddle and slips into Riddle Lake. Just as the B-Monster is about to go underwater, it lets out a huge, loud *bluuuuuurp*! An enormous gas bubble appears on the surface of the lake and it gets bigger and bigger and bigger until *kablam*! It pops.

I let out a crazy whoop.

"Slimo! Slimo! Slimo!"

"Calm down, calm down!" Ms. Shenanigans said, sounding exasperated. "Do any of you have questions for Mr. Block?"

I raised my hand up as high as I could. Here was my big chance to ask the long-burning question I had asked in all forty-eight of my letters.

Why did Oswald Leery hide up in his castle for seventeen years?

But drat if Walter didn't call on me. And he didn't he call on Lindsey either.

Kids rushed to a long table at the back of the room. Everyone pushed together to meet Walter face-to-face. He was passing out *Slimo* mini-posters.

Of course I couldn't squeeze in to talk to him. By now I'd lost track of Lindsey, too. And my watch said eight-thirty, which meant it was time to meet Dad.

I had to go.

Disappointed, I nudged my way through the throng away from Walter's table and toward the library exit. Ms. Shenanigans saw me leaving and said she'd save me a poster. On the way out, the *Slimo* theme song played inside my head.

Slimo's coming to our town!
Run before he slimes you down!
Fearsome fangs and glowing eyes!
Slimo takes you by surprise!
There's no escaping from the goo . . .
Especially not for you!

Even though I hadn't gotten to meet Leery or ask my questions, it had still been a pretty decent night.

"Jesse! Here!"

Dad was waiting in the car across the street from the library, just like he said.

He waved up to me. I took off, down the steps, running as fast as I could.

Thunk.

At the bottom step, I took an unplanned nosedive. My shoelaces were untied again.

As I struggled to get up, a black stretch limousine screeched to a stop *inches* from my head. A tinted window rolled down.

"My heavens! Are you okay?" a man asked.

I blinked twice. It was Walter Block!

"How did you get down here so fast?" I asked.

"No trouble at all," Walter replied.

He held out a silver-blue sealed envelope. On the front was my full name written in loopy, fancy letters: *Master Jesse Angus Ranger*

"For you, from the desk of Oswald Leery," Walter said, shoving the envelope into my hands.

Before I could respond, his window rolled back up and the limousine sped out of the parking lot.

Dad came running over just then. He had seen my fall on the bottom step.

"What happened?" Dad sounded concerned.

"Jesse, are you okay? Let me look at you. Did you get hurt?"

I didn't know what to say. My side ached. My palm was scratched up. I was more confused than anything else.

"How did Walter get out of here so fast?" I said again. I rubbed my head.

"Who was that?" Dad asked. "What's that in your hand?" He pointed to the letter.

I held up the blue envelope. It shimmered in the moonlight.

"Dad, I think I finally got my letter from Oswald Leery."

ONE *BLUUURP* BEYOND

"Are you sure you're okay, Jess?" Dad asked as he started up our car. "That looked like a bad fall."

I had a skinned knee, but that wasn't the worst thing. What felt really bad was my stomach. It was twisted into knots with nerves. I had waited an entire year for the envelope in my lap.

"Tear it open!" Dad said. "Let's see what's inside."

I wasn't sure what I was waiting for. I ripped open the envelope and pulled out a handwritten letter. I held it out in front of me, mentally preparing for the secrets. All of the answers to my B-Monster questions were waiting for me on this piece of paper—I just knew it!

"Well?" Dad said, turning to me as we pulled into our driveway. "Holy guacamole, Jesse! Would you *please* quit stalling? If you're not going to read it, I will."

"Dad," I said. "I just need a minute."

Dad parked the car and turned off the motor.

Slowly, I began to read the blue paper aloud.

Dear Jesse,

Due to circumstances beyond my control, I was unable to meet you in person at the Riddle Library tonight. Thank you for coming. I have read your many letters, Mr. Ranger. You are a B-Monster expert.

Although my plans took me out of town for the screening of Slimo, I will return home soon. Won't you please come for a personal tour of my castle?

My associate Mr. Walter Block will meet you at the front entrance this Friday at 3:30 P.M. I have invited four special fans, including yourself. Please be prompt.

Your friend,
Dr. Oswald Leery

"Wow!" Dad cheered. "A personal note *and* an invitation to the castle? That's too much!"

"Leery called me Mr. Ranger," I said, giggling. "*Your* name, Dad!"

My skin flushed all over. This *was* too much.

We walked into the kitchen. Mom was sitting at the wooden table with her briefcase and cell phone. The *Crabzilla* DVD case was there, too.

"So how was the library?" Mom asked.

"They showed *Slimo*," I said.

Dad grinned at me. He'd already called Mom to fill her in on all the details.

"What was it like to finally meet your favorite director, Oswald Leery?" Mom asked.

I shook my head. "I didn't meet him," I said. "We met his assistant Walter Block. He gave me this."

I held the silver-blue envelope so Mom could read it.

"Well," Mom said, taking it and quickly giving it a look. I could tell when she got to the part about the castle tour. Her eyes got all buggy.

"Well." Mom sighed. "This is something else."

"Yeah, too bad I can't go, right?" I said, hanging my head down and expecting the worst.

Mom looked right into my eyes. "Aw, Jess, you don't want to miss this, do you?"

"I don't?" My mouth curled into a grin. "No way, Mom."

"It's the opportunity of a lifetime," Mom said.

Inside, I was screaming for joy, but I made Mom say yes, of course I could go, *twice* more—just to be sure. I threw my arms around her shoulders and squeezed.

"Okay, enough hugs. Let's get upstairs, champ," Dad said. "We'll celebrate tomorrow."

I raced to my room and flipped onto my bed. The constellations poster on my ceiling glowed softly, and there I was, under it, King of the B-Monster galaxy.

I could go! I could go! I COULD GO!

Wow, did I need to rest. But there was no sleeping now. It felt like I'd eaten four ice cream sundaes and had a thousand shock waves powered directly to my brain. *And* I was thirsty.

I headed to the kitchen to get something to drink. Shadows covered the kitchen walls. I loved how the house looked at night, quiet and sleepy.

If only I felt sleepy!

I turned on the faucet for a cup of water. Nothing came out. I leaned in for a closer look. Sometimes things got stuck in the faucet. I flipped on the garbage disposal. I tried both faucet handles. I leaned down to check the pipes under the sink.

Bluuurp.

Without warning, the sink above me burped. It sounded and smelled like trapped air, or *me* after too many chili dogs. I stood right up.

Bluuurp.

A green bubble popped and the whole kitchen stank even worse now—like soccer socks. I pinched my nose. What kind of burp was *that*?

Another bubble came up from the sink. There was goo oozing out of the faucet and into the sink basin.

"This can't be real," I told myself, blinking. "What *is* that nasty stuff?"

I reached out to touch it but then jumped back. *Blecch!* I swiped a towel off the stove and rubbed my hands to get off the sticky. This was no ordinary goop. This looked exactly like—

SLIMO!

CHAPTER 5

THE GREAT FLOOD

Bluuurp.

I leaned close again.

Peeeeuw!

This really *was* Slimo.

Before I could really do anything, like shut the drain guard, the gross goo sucked itself back down into the pipes under the sink.

"Mom! Dad! Come quick!" I wailed. I clicked off the kitchen lights so I wouldn't have to look at it. I could still hear this gurgling, rushing sound, and my feet and pajamas were starting to get wet. Eww! The goo must be overflowing onto the floor! I screamed again. "Mom! Dad! HELP!"

The two of them rushed into the kitchen a few moments later, rubbing their eyes.

"What's the matter, Jesse?" Mom asked. "Are you okay?"

Dad yawned. He looked like one of Oswald Leery's Zoltan Zombies standing there. They're the undead B-Monsters brought back to life by the evil Dr. Zoltan in *Zattack of the Zombies.* They are at the top of my list of best bad dudes *ever*.

"This better be good," Dad grunted.

"Umm . . . something's wrong with the sink," I warned. I could still hear the dripping.

Dad flicked on the kitchen light switch. Mom let out a shriek.

"Oh!" she cried.

Dad groaned. "Jesse!"

The kitchen was a flood zone. Water ran down the counter and onto the floor like a waterfall! We stood in a large puddle that covered nearly half of the kitchen's tiled surface.

Water, water everywhere. But no slime *anywhere.* I knew I was in big trouble with my parents, but I didn't care. I was just relieved to see water on the floor instead of slime.

"What happened?" Mom cried. She was wide

awake now. "Don't you know how to turn off the faucet? Look at this disaster!"

"No! Wait!" I said. "A minute ago this wasn't water. There was something else in the sink. It was green—"

"Jesse Ranger!" Dad barked at me. "Stop making excuses! Go and get some towels!"

"Dad, I swear, there really was something else coming out of the faucet. It was green, just like Slimo, I *swear*!"

"Slimo?" Dad said, incredulous.

"JESSE ANGUS RANGER!" Mom let out an exasperated sigh. "B-Monsters are NOT real! Get to bed. Now!"

I looked over at Dad, desperate for a little backup. But he was on his hands and knees, mopping up the mess with dish towels. He looked up at me with one of those "you're on your own, kid" looks.

I bolted back upstairs to my room.

How could this have happened? I asked myself. I went over the last ten minutes inside my head. I'd turned on the faucet to find the source of the *bluuurp*. Had I forgotten to turn it back the other way? That must have been why the water kept running.

I was more confused than ever.

And I was still thirsty.

I went into my bathroom, grabbed a paper cup, and turned on the water.

At first, everything was normal. The faucet turned on with no problems and the water ran clear. But then, out of nowhere, it gushed this green, thick goop, all at once! Just like the stuff in the downstairs kitchen!

Quickly, I turned off the faucet and closed my eyes tight.

Sluuurp.

Everything sucked back down the drain again. I quickly checked the faucet. I didn't want to flood the bathroom, too.

"That didn't just happen, that didn't just happen," I told myself.

I pulled the bathroom door open, backed into my room, clicked off the overhead light, and dove under my covers.

"That didn't just happen, that didn't just happen," I repeated.

Cautiously, I peeked over the edge of my blanket. The bathroom door was still open just a crack. At first I could hardly see anything, it was so dark. But then I saw something: a neon green, quivering glow.

It was getting brighter. And there was that smell. The same one from the kitchen.

I took a gulp of air and counted to three. Then I jumped out from under the covers and dashed across the bedroom. The creepy green light was definitely coming from the bathroom.

I wanted to yell for Mom and Dad again, but I knew I shouldn't.

I *couldn't.*

With all my might, I threw my body against the bathroom door. As it flew open, I threw on the overhead light.

Za-zzzap! The lightbulb sizzled.

The green was gone!

Now there wasn't a single drop of slime *anywhere.* And it smelled normal again, like those powder-fresh air fresheners Mom plugs into the wall.

Somehow, Slimo had disappeared again!

CHAPTER 6

MY TEACHER IS MISSING!

"Your attention, please. The third floor of the building has been closed, effective immediately. Students are restricted from this area and the upper gym. Classes have been relocated to the library and first-floor assembly rooms. Thank you," Principal Pickle's nasal voice droned over the intercom the next morning at school.

The halls buzzed. Kids clumped together, whispering in groups. Something was going on. No one knew what it was, but I could tell it had to be BIG.

"Jess!" Garth grabbed my shoulder in the hall outside the locker bank. "Did you hear that announcement?"

"Yeah," I said.

"Maybe spaceships landed on the roof!" Garth teased me.

"Spaceships?" I quipped. "Let's go upstairs and see what it *really* is."

Garth made a face. "Are you kidding?"

"Come on! Don't you want a logical explanation for all this chaos?" I said, appealing to the scientist in Garth.

He fell for the bait—and agreed to head for the third floor.

"I'm only doing this because . . ." Garth mumbled. "Hey, why *am* I doing this?"

"Maybe something exploded," I said.

"Nah," Garth said, making a face. "If that were true, we would have heard the actual explosion."

Just then, some guy hustled past us with a very big video camera. The back of his shirt said NEWS 12.

"Whoa," Garth said. "That must be serious."

"Where's he going?" I wondered aloud.

"Third floor," Garth said. "The place we're not supposed to go. Remember?"

"Hurry up before we lose him!"

Out of the corner of my eye, I saw Principal Pickle waving his arms all over the place.

"Out of the way! Clear the halls!" he cried.

We dodged out of the way. Coming down the

hall behind Principal Pickle was Security Guard Spiker. Three police officers barreled down the hall with him.

"Get to class, kids," Principal Pickle yelled as he ran.

"That means *you*," Spiker barked at Garth and me as he and the police went by.

Garth looked at me. I looked at Garth. We broke into nervous giggles.

"Come on," I pleaded, watching them head up the main stairs.

"Come on *what*?" Garth cried.

"Let's follow them," I said. "We can take the side stairs instead."

Garth pursed his lips. I knew he was going to say *no*. And then he surprised me.

"Okay," Garth blurted. "But just for a second."

We ignored the class bell, sidestepped the other kids lurking in the hall, and slipped into a side stairwell.

The walk up to the third floor took only a few seconds. We took two stairs at a time. At the top, Garth cracked open a heavy door. We peeked out.

"Cops!" I whispered. "They're everywhere."

I could see them telling the guy from *NEWS 12* to go back downstairs.

Garth tugged on my shirt. "I don't like this," he said. "We're going to get caught."

"No, we won't!" I said. "There's a bathroom around the corner. We can make a break for it."

"What if the door's locked?" Garth asked.

"It won't be!" I cried, shoving him. "Come on!"

We both ran as fast as we could, past a water fountain, closed classrooms, and a huge garbage can, and then ducked into the bathroom.

"*That* was wicked!" I exclaimed, hopping up onto a sink ledge.

"Yeah, that was wicked, all right," Garth said. "Wicked *stupid*. They could have seen us! Now what do we do?"

I looked around for a way out. That's when I saw feet in one of the bathroom stalls. My gut twisted into a knot. We weren't *alone*?

"Yo, Ranger!" a voice said from the stall. "That you?"

I cringed. Not *again*. The stall door slammed open and Damon Molloy, Enemy Number One, walked out with two of his backup posse. I have all the luck.

"Who invited you two to our stakeout?" Damon cracked.

I groaned. "Who invited *you*?"

"Whoa," Damon snapped, crossing his arms. He flicked at my ear. "This is *our* stakeout. Not yours. Scram."

"We can't go back out there!" Garth babbled. "There are cops out there."

"Cops?" Damon looked surprised. "What cops?"

"Outside. Right now," I said.

"Whoa!" Damon said. "I guess Principal Pickle called the police once he realized our teacher was missing," Damon said.

"A teacher is missing?" I asked. "Who?"

"Mr. Bunsen vanished into thin air this morning, moron," Damon replied. "Where have *you* been? Under a rock?"

"Mr. Bunsen?" I said.

"Yeah, the teacher with the secret briefcase," Damon said. We made fun of Mr. Bunsen on a regular basis. He had crazy silver hair and always wore lab coats and these ugly blue and green sneakers.

"I heard he's an undercover spy," said one of the kids in Damon's posse.

51

"And I heard he's billionaire rich with a hidden laboratory," said another one.

"Are you guys serious?" I asked.

My head reeled. I had heard loads of Riddle rumors about Mr. Bunsen and some of the other teachers before now. I always wondered if there was any truth to them. And what about the night before,

when I saw Mr. Bunsen on the library steps? What did *that* mean?

Just then we heard a sound in the hall. Someone was opening the bathroom door!

Garth cried, "The cops!" but I held my hand over his mouth. The five of us panicked, crammed into the biggest bathroom stall, and then waited.

And waited.

But no one came in.

"There are no cops coming, dorkus," Damon growled at Garth.

"So now what?" I asked.

"We should go scope out Bunsen's classroom," Damon suggested.

Brrrrrrrrrrrrrring.

The second-period bell rang. We didn't have much time.

Damon puffed out his chest and shoved me forward. "Move it or lose it," he ordered, poking Garth and me in our backs. We were like his human shields as we ducked back into the hall. I half-expected Spiker or the cops to jump us. But the hall was empty.

We walked toward Mr. Bunsen's classroom.

"Ewww, do you smell that?" Damon said.

"Whew," I gasped. It smelled like armpits or my Dad's old sneakers. But Garth said he didn't smell anything.

We approached the doorway slowly, just in case someone was there. But we were alone. The cops were gone—at least for now.

As we stepped into the room, I couldn't believe my eyes. There was slime all over! The entire science lab—walls, floor, ceiling—was splattered with some kind of goo. It stank *bad*.

"Where do you think all this slime came from?" I whispered to Garth.

"What slime?" Garth said.

I made a sour face. "Are you kidding me? What do you mean *what slime*? It's all over the place. Can't you see it? Can't you *smell* that?"

Garth frowned and looked inside again. "*What* slime?" he said. "All I see in Mr. Bunsen's room are lab tables and a big mess of papers."

I saw Damon listening to us. He leaned over to his own friends.

"Dudes," Damon asked them. "See all the slime on the wall?"

Both guys shook their heads. "No."

"*That* slime. On the walls?" Damon said, his voice rising. "RIGHT THERE! DON'T YOU SEE THAT?!"

"Shhh!" I cried softly. But it was too late. The pack of cops had heard our voices. I could hear them stomping back down the hall. They did *not* look happy to see us.

My whole body shook. *Were they going to arrest us? What was the punishment for trespassing on the third floor? Would I live to see another day?*

Garth and the posse ducked out of the classroom. But I didn't move.

Neither did Damon.

Spiker came into the classroom first. He made a sour face at me. "Jesse," Spiker groaned. "You shouldn't be here."

"Yeah, you kids better head to class before you're sent to the principal's office," a cop said sternly, pointing his sausagelike finger at us.

"This floor is way off-limits," another cop growled. "There's nothing to see."

"Nothing but a whole truckload of slime, right?" I muttered.

"Slime? What slime?" Spiker asked.

"*That* green slime," Damon said. "Don't you see it?"

"There's no slime here!" the third cop said. "Now you better get moving before you start seeing little green men, too."

I gulped. Why could we see the slime when no one else could?

"Okay, boys, I'm taking you in," the first cop said. "You're going to get into big, BIG trouble. I wouldn't be surprised if you got expelled for—"

"Hold on," Spiker interrupted. "I know these kids."

The cop stepped back.

Spiker waved his hand down the hall. "Shove off, kids. Before I change my mind . . ."

Before we turned away, Damon nudged me in the side. "Ranger," he whispered. I could barely hear him. "Look at that!"

I glanced into Mr. Bunsen's classroom. In a corner near the teacher's desk was a pair of blue-green sneakers just like the ones I had seen on Mr. Bunsen's feet a day before. What were those doing there?

Near Mr. Bunsen's shoes, a strange puddle of slime caught my attention.

It had spelled out a word right there on the floor.

BEWARE.

"Let's get out of here!" I cried as we took off down the hall.

CHAPTER 7

THE NINJA KNOWS

Damon and I bolted back into the stairwell. We were both sweating bullets.

"That stuff in the classroom was turning into Slimo for real!" I gasped, taking two steps down at a time. "It's just like Oswald Leery's B-Monster movies! Once the monster gets its teeth, it will eat us all!"

"Why didn't anyone besides you and me see the slime?" Damon asked.

"I don't know," I whispered back. "That goo was *everywhere*."

"I saw slime last night, too," Damon said in a low voice.

I stopped short. "You did?"

"I woke up in the middle of the night drooling so I went into the bathroom to wash my face. But when

I picked up the towel by the sink, it was covered in this green, sticky, stinky goo."

"Ewwww," I groaned. "That's *snot* possible!" I cracked, making a lame joke. I do that sometimes when I'm feeling nervous.

Of course Damon shot me an evil stare. "This isn't funny, dorkus!"

"I'm not laughing," I said, even though I was. "The truth is, I saw slime, too. It came out of our kitchen sink."

"The sink? Just like mine!" Damon cried.

"It's a sign," I said.

"Right," Damon said. "A sign that we're doomed."

We headed back to our regular classroom. We were so late! Ms. Sharp would probably throw a fit. But when we went through the door, the teacher wasn't even there! Kids were talking and goofing off.

Lindsey looked up and waved from the back row.

"Jesse, what are you doing with *him*?" she asked, rolling her eyes at Damon.

"Long story," I said. "Did you know that Mr. Bunsen disappeared?"

"Disappeared? What?" Lindsey's eyes popped open. "From where?" she blinked.

"From his classroom. In fact, we were just upstairs looking at—"

"Ranger!" Damon grabbed my shoulder hard. His voice sounded panicked. "What if Ms. Sharp disappeared, too? What if this is some kind of sneaky alien invasion like the one in *Martian Mayhem*?"

That was one of my least favorite B-Monster movies, but I was impressed by the reference. Maybe Damon knew more about Bs than I thought.

"What's the matter with you guys?" Lindsey chuckled. "Ms. Sharp didn't disappear. She went out into the hall with Principal Pickle. I mean, she's been gone a while now, but . . ."

"Lindsey, something is really wrong around here," I said.

"Is it any more wrong than any other day?" Lindsey asked. "Don't worry so much. Ms. Sharp will be right back. She said so."

Sure enough, Ms. Sharp walked in a moment later. Damon and I dove for our seats.

"Hello, students!" Ms. Sharp declared. "I'm back at last! There will be no more interruptions. Take out your math books. I think we can salvage some of this lesson."

Math? *Now?* It was going to be hard to concentrate for a whole ten minutes.

Something hit my shoulder with a ping. A paper airplane landed on the floor next to me. I twisted around to see who had launched it.

The Ninja!

Stella Min stared me down with her beady brown eyes. I'd forgotten she was in this class. Carefully, I opened the note on my lap.

I see the slime, too.

"Mr. Ranger?"

I gasped aloud. Ms. Sharp hovered over me.

"Is there something wrong, Mr. Ranger?" Ms. Sharp asked, raising an eyebrow. "I asked you a question."

"You did?" I stammered. "Uh . . . uh . . ."

How was I supposed to solve unit conversions and do pre-algebra at a time like this? I shouted out a random number.

"Three hundred and eleven."

Ms. Sharp sighed. "Good grief! You need to read the chapter again, Mr. Ranger," she groaned. She turned to Myles "Brain Boy" Boxer for the correct answer.

I whirled back around in my seat. A second piece of paper crash-landed on my desktop. This folded note looked like an origami bird.

I think we should talk. Look over here.

I glanced back at Stella. My heart sank.

In her hand, Stella held a shimmering blue piece of paper. She had an invitation just like the one Walter Block had given to me outside the library!

I gulped and leaned back into my bag. Where was my own blue invitation? I held it up high so Stella could see.

Then, out of the corner of my eye, I spotted Damon holding the very same blue piece of paper in his fist. His eyes flashed at me and then at Lindsey.

She had a blue paper, too?

Whoa.

We were the four kids invited to go to the castle?

Brrrrrrrrrring.

The class bell rang. The four of us raced for the door at the exact same time. We huddled in the hallway, away from the flow of traffic.

"I can't believe we each got these!" I said excitedly. "I can't believe we have so much in common . . ."

"Hold on, Ranger. I don't have *anything* in common with you," Damon said.

"Oh, brother," Lindsey frowned. "You are such an idiot, Damon Molloy!"

"Yeah, well . . . Mister Idiot to you," Damon cracked.

"Lindsey," I asked. "Did you see any slime yesterday?"

Lindsey squirmed a little bit. Her eyes went from me to Damon to Stella and back again. Then she finally confessed. Yes, she'd seen a bunch of slime in her backyard sprinklers!

"How did you know?" Lindsey asked.

I took a deep breath. All four of us had seen the slime. This was serious.

"Why is this happening?" I muttered.

"Duh! Because we like B-Monster movies," Damon said. "We're like Oswald Leery's own personal fan club or something."

"Nah. He has a trillion fans just like us," I said. "There has to be something more, something else . . ."

"Let's go up to Leery Castle on Friday like the invitation says," Stella said. "We can get to the bottom of all this."

"Are you nuts?" Damon cried. "You want to go see Leery Castle and Oswald Leery *for real*? The guy has to be a hundred years old and probably doesn't even know his own name. I am not going anywhere near that relic. Trust me. This slime thing has to be some kind of joke."

"Joke? What about Mr. Bunsen?" I said. "He's gone. That's no joke."

"He's not gone," Damon said. "He's just . . ."

"GONE!" Stella snapped. "Face it. There's some kind of slime on the loose and it decided to snack on our teacher! We're probably next!"

"We're the only ones who can see the slime. We have to help Mr. Bunsen. Otherwise, who else will?" I said, sounding braver than I felt. Mr. Bunsen was cool as far as teachers went. We couldn't just let the slime have him.

"Maybe Oswald Leery can help us find Mr. Bunsen and figure all this out," Lindsey suggested.

"Leery makes movies, not science," Damon said, laughing hard. "Slimo is a big green *movie star*, people! It's not real. It's movies."

"How can we be so sure?" Stella cried. She twirled the ends of her long hair and crossed her arms thoughtfully. "If there is a connection between Bunsen and the slime, Oswald Leery will know what it is. He invented Slimo. He chose the four of us for a very good reason."

Now we just had to figure out what the reason was.

CHAPTER 8

ON TOP OF NERVE MOUNTAIN

Friday came faster than I expected. I wanted to get ready for the trip up to Leery Castle, but Garth kept bugging me after school.

"Why can't you come over and play *Master of the Cosmos* with me?" Garth asked. "We always play video games together on Friday afternoons. What's the matter with you?"

"I have something to do," I said awkwardly.

"Like what? You never do anything exciting," Garth quipped.

"Thanks a lot," I said.

"Aw, you know what I mean," Garth said. "You've been acting weird for the past couple of days. Can't you tell me? I'm your best buddy."

I knew Garth was right, but I also knew that I had something important to do with Damon Molloy, Stella

Min, and Lindsey Gomez. I just wasn't sure what it was yet.

Just then, Stella walked over, looking tough. She was dressed all in black, as usual.

"Ranger, let's go," she growled at me.

Garth looked at me with a look of horror. Then he looked at Stella. Then he looked at me again.

"Are you ditching me for a girl, Jesse?" he asked.

I tried to explain, but Garth marched off in a major huff. I was going to have to spend a lot of time playing video games with him to make up for this.

Damon Molloy was hanging around the school playground with his crew, *literally*. I watched him climb all the way to the top of the jungle gym, pound his chest like a gorilla, and hang off the top bar by his knees.

On his T-shirt today was just one word: TUFF.

What a show-off, I thought.

Lindsey was hanging out at the main school building with her friends, including Desiree Payton, who is quite possibly the snooty-snootiest girl at Riddle Elementary School. Unlike Stella or me or even Damon, Lindsey seems to have an endless supply of friends. I wondered if they would still like her when they spotted her hanging out with all of us. Ha! They'd probably give her some kind of disintegrating death stare just like Dr. Zoltan in *Zattack of the Zombies*. That's what the snoots do best: blow you off.

I just hoped Lindsey kept her lips locked. Our big B-Monster secret could not get out to Desiree or anyone else at school! A little information in the wrong hands could jeopardize the entire operation.

Finally, Lindsey left her friends and came over to the bus stop where we were waiting. As we boarded the bus, the sky started to cloud over. It looked like it was going to be a rainy night.

The bus chugged up the road, past the Glog Glen Diner, across Gravesend Ridge, and all the way up to the very top of Nerve Mountain. Still no rain.

At the top, a barbed wire fence appeared along the side of the road, covered with kooky signs like B-CAREFUL! and B-WARE OF MONSTERS! I guessed that Oswald Leery had put up those signs a very long time ago, back when he used to give tours of his castle.

As the bus pulled up to a stop near the top I saw a sign that read: LEERY CASTLE.

"You know this old place is closed," the driver said, leaning on the DOOR OPEN lever for the bus. "Has been shut up for years."

I smirked. "We know. We wanted to see it anyway."

"Suit yourself," the driver said. He shut the door and motored away.

"I wish I had a camera," I said, eyeing the sign again.

"I do!" Lindsey cried. She took out her camera and got us into position.

Damon, Stella, and I posed next to the Leery Castle sign.

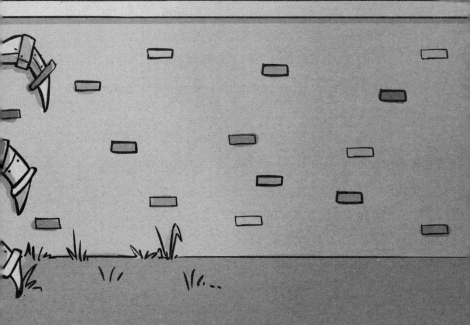

Then we posed near the castle gates. Rising high over our heads were two enormous Crabzilla gates with strong, supersized iron claws. The gates looked even scarier against the backdrop of a stormy sky.

Lindsey snapped a few more photos.

"When I started watching Oswald Leery movies at my parents' drive-in theater, I never imagined something as crazy as *this*," Damon said, looking around.

"Hold on! Your parents run the Desert Drive-O-Rama?" I asked. "And you've never been up here before?"

Damon shook his head. "Dad said I couldn't come up until I was ten."

"That was last year," Stella said. "Maybe you didn't come up because you were *afraid*!"

"No!" Damon said. "I just didn't feel like it."

All at once, the intercom sizzled. We heard a scratchy voice.

"Hello there! I've been expecting you!" Walter said. "Press the code to come through the gates. It's *Slimo*."

We looked at each other.

"Slimo?" Damon looked worried.

The wind whipped around us and I got goose bumps all over. Then I saw the keypad with letters.

Damon punched the letters. The moment he hit the *O* in *Slimo*, we heard something crunch inside one of the Crabzilla legs. The two Crabzilla gates began to shift and twist. Their enormous claws opened and then closed slowly, like nutcrackers.

Screeeeeeeech.

We hurried inside the gates quickly, afraid the claws might clamp down and turn us into crab cakes.

"There's the front door!" Lindsey cried. I saw it, too. It was up ahead, past the mess of brambles and plaster garden sculptures. Models of all the best B-Monsters could be found on this pathway, molded in plastic with chipped but brightly colored paint jobs: Bog Beast, Smog Thing, Space Leech, and others.

"Watch out for booby traps," Damon warned.

"Why would there be booby traps here?" I asked.

Damon shrugged. "You never know. There are always booby traps in the movies."

Lindsey and Stella found an oversize stepping stone in the shape of Rodiak's foot.

She started snapping photos again: a shot of the Rodiak footprint; a close-up of Damon, Stella, and me under some creepy-looking vines; a shot of another great big sign that read: ENTER AT YOUR OWN RISK. A thunderbolt cracked over our heads. The rain was coming closer. What were we going to do if it poured?

"Hey! Look at the door!" Lindsey cried.

We all looked. It was *open*.

It hadn't been open a minute ago.

"Hello?" I called out, walking inside cautiously.

"Hello? Walter? Professor Leery?" Damon called out after me. He and the girls followed me in. The door slammed shut behind us. We all jumped.

"Mr. Leery?" I yelled.

There was no answer.

Spread out before us was a sweeping, swerving staircase covered in deep purple plush carpet. The only sounds I heard were the bubbling of a fish tank somewhere and the tick-tock of an enormous grandfather clock. It was dark and the ceilings were lost in shadows.

The wide foyer was tiled in checkered marble, but it didn't look as elegant as you would think. It was a real mess. There were too many shelves and tables covered with stuff like teddy bears with fangs and pillows with strange maps. There was a row of funny hats and masks and rubber boots. Framed bats with wings had been displayed in neat cases along the bottom of the stairs. A large black stuffed crow was perched on the banister. It wore a jeweled collar.

"Hello?" Stella called out. No one answered.

Butterflies sprang up in my stomach. I was beginning to think that coming here had been a bad idea.

"We should go," Damon whispered. "Like, *now*."

"What happened to 'tuff'?" Stella teased, pointing to his T-shirt. "I thought you'd be the first one to stick around and beat up a few monsters!"

Caw, caw, caw!

Before Damon could answer, the black crow that had been sitting on the banister opened its beak! It stretched out its wide black wings and lifted up off the stairs.

Lindsey looked panicked. "It's not stuffed!" she cried.

Stella struck a karate pose and chopped at the air. "Keep back, bird!" she said.

Damon hit the floor.

I didn't know what to do. The crow flapped its wings and flew toward us. I grabbed a folded-up newspaper that was lying on a table and swatted at the air.

"Jesse! Look out!" Lindsey cried.

The crow was perched high on a bookshelf, but it was staring right at me.

Caw, caw, caw!

The crow flapped up again and flew in a quick circle over my head. Then it flew up into the shadows.

"What's it doing now?" Damon asked. He was lying flat on the floor with his arms over his head.

"Forget the crow," Stella joked. "Meet the chicken."

I reached out to help Damon up when suddenly Stella knocked us both back down again.

"Watch out!" Stella yelled as she fell on top of us. "Incoming!"

I looked up just in time to see the crow take a nosedive straight for my head!

CHAPTER 9

DANGER MAN

"Duck!" Stella cried to me. "DUUUUUCK!"

I darted to the side to avoid a head-on collision.

"Hey, it's a crow, not a duck," Lindsey cracked to Stella and me.

"NO MORE BIRD JOKES!" I cried.

Stella wasn't laughing but Lindsey still was. Sometimes I think Lindsey has a permanent case of the giggles.

Caw, caw, caw!

Why was the crow so determined to chase after me? I wondered.

"Watch out, Jesse! He must like you!" Lindsey cried out.

A whistle came from afar. Walter Block appeared.

77

"Over here, Poe," Walter called to the bird. "Stay."

And just like that, the crow perched on Walter's shoulder.

"That was way too close," I said to Walter. I collapsed onto one of the velvet sofas in the room.

"Can I get up now?" Damon said, peeking out.

"Yes," Walter said. "Meet Poe, the mascot of Leery Castle."

"Poe? Like Edgar Allan Poe?" Stella asked.

"Indeed." Walter nodded. "Follow us," he continued, moving with the crow into the adjoining room.

The room was round with huge wooden doors every few feet or so. I'd never seen anything like it. In the center of the room were two massive sofas, assorted chairs, and tables. There were candles, coasters, magazines, cups, saucers, bric-a-brac, and dust (of course) covering every available surface. There was even a stuffed tarantula on the top of the sofa, and coffee table books with alien art on the front stacked next to a chair.

Walter led us to a table with bowls and cups on it. "Here are some snacks and drinks for you," he said. There were chilled cans of Volt Cola lined up like bowling pins.

Damon grabbed a handful of cheesy-looking mix. Orange stuff got all over his fingers and lips. Stella and Lindsey took huge handfuls, too.

"Mmmmm," the girls said. "What *is* this?"

"One of Oswald Leery's favorites," said Walter. "Larva crunch."

"Ewwwwww!" everyone wailed, spitting the stuff out. *"Larva?"*

"Oh, come now! You're not afraid of a little snack food, are you?" Walter asked.

Stella grabbed a can of Volt Cola right off the tray

and emptied it into her mouth. It would take a case of the stuff to get the taste out of our mouths.

"Would you excuse me for a moment?" Walter asked. "Have a look around. Make yourselves at home. I'll be back in two shakes of a werewolf's tail."

Then he left the room.

"How exactly do you shake a werewolf's tail?" I cried.

"*Very carefully*," Lindsey said, giggling again as she adjusted her glasses.

We all groaned.

"What does it mean when Walter says to 'have a look around'?" Stella asked, touching a large, leather-bound book on the table.

"I bet he's testing us," I said. "He wants to see what we do."

"I bet Leery has B-Monster video cams set up all over the castle," said Damon. "We'll probably end up on the Internet."

Stella found a box and opened it up. Inside were old pictures of actors, special-effects design people, and makeup artists who had worked at B-Monster Studios. Dad told me once that a bunch of old

B-Monster actors still live at the Riddle Retirement Village. I bet they have the best stories to tell!

Hidden behind a large, moving plywood panel, Damon discovered shelves and shelves of back issues of *B-Monster Galaxy*, Oswald Leery's famed monster magazine. On another shelf was a giant robot head. Damon stepped near the head and its eyes flashed red.

"Cool!" he exclaimed excitedly.

Lindsey pointed to a line of old black-and-white photographs hanging up on the wall. In one photograph was a man behind a movie camera. Standing next to the man was Oswald Leery.

"Wow! That man in the picture is my Grandpa Max!" Lindsey said.

I told Lindsey how my Great Uncle Rich had worked for Leery, too.

"His nickname was Danger Ranger," I joked. "Otherwise known as Danger Man."

"Where is he in these pictures?" Damon asked, eyeing all the photographs again.

I searched the gallery and couldn't find a photo of him anywhere. But I didn't need a photograph. I found some amazing props instead! Inside a costume trunk, I picked up this bug mask with giant light-up eyes. Etched inside was the name RICH "D" RANGER

"No way!" Damon cried. "Look at this!" He pulled me over to look at a gigantic suit made of steel. "It says right here that this suit was worn by Rich Ranger in *Robototron*."

"Wow," Stella said. "There are little bits of your uncle in everything."

"Yeah," I mused. "He was a cool guy, wasn't he?"

"When I grow up, I want to be a stuntwoman just like him," Stella said.

"You could be 'Danger Min'!" I cried, goofing around.

We all laughed, except for Stella, of course. She smoothed down her black hair and shot me a look. "I'm being serious," she said.

I spotted a small locked cabinet off to the side of the room. Unable to open it, I grabbed a sharpened pencil and stuck it in the lock. After a few minutes of wriggling, the door opened.

The cabinet was a treasure trove. It held notebooks and albums crammed with photos and facts, guestbooks signed by all the actors who had made the Bs, and a box of original B-Monster trading cards. I opened the box. I'd been searching for a limited-edition *Slimo* trading card for months. There were only five ever issued. Two are owned by collectors in Japan, and I had no clue where the other three might be.

Unfortunately, Oswald Leery didn't have one in this box.

"I wonder where all the doors in this room go," Damon said.

Lindsey reached for one knob, but Stella cried, "Don't! You don't know what's behind there!"

"Isn't that the idea?" Lindsey said with a smile. She moved over to a curious-looking set of yellow double doors.

The plaque on the doors read: SCREENING ROOM.

With a loud crank, the yellow double doors started to move. They were on some kind of mechanical track and they were opening themselves in slo-mo.

I stepped forward before everyone else. It was pitch-black inside.

I couldn't even see my hand in front of my face!

As I moved inside the room, everything wobbled and before I could find my bearings, the entire floor gave way.

Before I could stop myself, I was falling down, down into the darkness.

CHAPTER 10

DOCTOR LEERY, I PRESUME?

I screamed as I fell. It was so dark that I couldn't even see where I had fallen. Then suddenly I bounced against something slippery. This was a slide!

As I twisted down the loop, I squealed like I was on a roller coaster. I could feel wind on my eyeballs. This was like the best amusement park ride *ever*. I was beginning to wonder if it would ever stop.

And then it did.

Just as quickly as I'd dropped onto the slide, I was deposited into a plush chair facing an enormous screen. I was in some kind of futuristic movie theater! There was a creaking noise, and the chair lurched and moved over a little. Stella, who had dropped down after me, was positioned in a chair to my left. She just stared ahead like she'd been hypnotized or something. Or maybe she was just completely freaked out.

I know I was.

On the right side of me, another chair slid into place under the slide chute. Then Lindsey came sliding down into it. Damon slipped into another chair after her.

I always thought the multiplex in Riddle was impressive. After all, it has something like twelve different screens. But the theater at Leery Castle put that place to super-shame. This screening room was WOW all the way.

Our chairs were positioned so close to the screen, I figured we could practically see the actors' nose hair. Obviously, that was the best way to view any Bs. The closer, the grosser, the better the B! I remember reading that somewhere once in an old issue of *B-Monster Galaxy* magazine. It sounded like a cheer.

As the lights inside the screening room faded to a pale glint, a face popped up on the screen.

Oswald Leery!

"Welcome to my castle, Jesse, Stella, Damon, and Lindsey. I am sorry that I cannot be with you today," Leery said.

His voice echoed. I glanced around. I could barely see in the darkness, but I knew the four of us had the same exact facial expression: freaked. Leery was up there, saying our names and talking directly to us!

"My friends, our beloved town of Riddle is in grave danger," Leery continued. "Back in the days before my family started making movies here, Riddle was a simple town. No one worried much about danger or horror. But when I invented B-Monster Vision, something strange happened. Riddle changed. Everything changed. For all these many years, I have guarded a deep secret."

I sank down into my chair. Secret? I loved secrets!

"Let me start at the beginning," Leery said. "I want you to understand a little bit about my world."

Grainy old photos of Desmond and Lucas Leery projected onto the oversize screen. We saw photos of old movie sets and actors dressed in all sorts of funny costumes. Then we saw grown-up photos of Leery directing on the very same movie sets we knew. Photos from *Crabzilla*, *Tuskadon*, and *Bog Beast* flashed on-screen. The B-Monsters looked fun and fake, of course, just the way they always had.

"I grew up on movies," Leery's voice narrated as the photos faded one into the other. "My father and grandfather before him were masters of cinema. I spent all of my time on movie sets and learned the tricks of camera work, makeup, and more from them. When I got older, I started to make movies on my own. That's when I started using the filming process my grandfather and father had invented. I gave it my own name: B-Monster Vision."

I pressed the small of my back into the chair as I listened and watched the photographs flashing before me. I thought I knew everything there was to know about Leery, but I only knew very little. There was so much to learn!

"One day," Leery went on, "I realized that my B-Monster Vision was causing problems on the sets of my movies. Things began to disappear. Sets were destroyed by mysterious rain or even slime . . ."

"Slime?" Lindsey gasped. I couldn't see, but I knew that was her voice in the dark. My eyes fixed back on the screen.

"My colleagues and I realized that the unthinkable was taking place right here at B-Monster Studios. Somehow B-Monsters were being *made* real by the very camera I had used to put them in the movies."

I grabbed the edge of the cushion on the chair where I was sitting. *This has to be a joke*, I told myself.

"My young friends," Leery continued. "Not only are B-Monsters real, but they are trapped in the original copies of the movies. So, each time an original copy of a film is screened, that B-Monster comes alive again."

"For years, I tried to fight these Bs," Leery continued. "I tried swords and armor and even acid. I tried chants and spells. But nothing—*nothing*—has worked. Just when I think I've stopped a monster, it comes back again. Or a new monster strikes . . ."

My stomach was in knots. I wanted to run, but I didn't even know where the ground was under my seat! Leery was still talking.

"My crew and I were able to contain the damage, but only for short periods of time. I began making sequels to my greatest movies to put the real B-Monsters back to work. It kept them contained—for a while. The public loved the sequels. So I just made more and more movies."

I laughed aloud. He put monsters *to work*. This was too much!

"However, as time passed, I grew tired," Leery said. I could see the tiredness in his eyes up on the screen. "B-Monsters were getting smarter. I couldn't control them anymore. They wanted to run free in Riddle—and beyond. They wanted to get out. Making movies with them was not enough to keep them away from trouble. I locked the gates of the castle. I put away all the cameras. I went back into my castle, into hiding. I needed to stop the B-Monsters for good."

Up on the screen, Oswald Leery got very still. He stared directly at the camera and breathed a raspy, eerie breath. He sounded like one of his own special effects.

"To destroy a B-Monster, two important things must happen. Each monster must be controlled and then eliminated. Then you must destroy the original copy of that B-Monster movie!"

Leery stared out at us, as if he were waiting for some kind of response. He blinked slowly. "Do you understand?" he asked as if he were speaking in real time.

"Unfortunately, it took me years to figure out that last part. And I wasn't very careful with the original reels. I had sent them to fans and friends all over the world. I have no idea who has what or which films I sent where. I have tracked down many of the original reels," he went on, "but there is no way I can find them all on my own. Not now. That's where *you* come in."

The room got awfully quiet. Stella, Lindsey, Damon, and I were too shocked to breathe.

"I need the four of you to help me. I planned the screening at the library as a way to get you together. I had Walter give your librarian a list of VIP names. You were on that list with other children, but you four were the ones I needed most."

Could I have seen this coming? I knew there

was something fishy about that VIP list! I never would have guessed in a zillion years that Oswald Leery would want *my* help to eliminate an actual B-Monster!

"Together, I need your help to locate my entire catalog of original B-Monster movies. Some are right here in Riddle. Others may be halfway across the world. And owners won't always be willing to part with them. But we must find them all!"

Leery moved closer to the camera.

"There is one more thing!" he cried. My stomach wrenched. Now I really could see his nose hair. I could almost feel him breathing on me.

"I know you will guard my secret, the secret of the Bs," Leery said. "But be careful who you talk to! There will be people who know things about the monsters. They will help you along the way. But you, Jesse, Damon, Stella, and Lindsey, *you* are the true Monster Squad."

All at once, static filled the screen. The camera sizzled.

POOF!

Oswald Leery was gone.

CHAPTER 11

SMELLS LIKE FEET

The lights inside the screening room blared on. I realized that I had squeezed my chair's armrests so tightly that my fingers had gone completely numb. The truth was, I felt numb all over. None of us said a word. Could it all possibly be true?

Walter reappeared. He strode to a small platform in front of the enormous screen.

"Any questions?" he asked.

Still no one said a word.

"Come now!" Walter said. "You must have questions."

"This is some kind of crazy hoax!" Damon cried.

Walter Block shook his head. "No, this is real, my friends. Dr. Leery recorded that message for you just two weeks ago. He was on a remote island in the South Pacific Ocean, searching for *Mega Mantis*, who escaped again after the original film had been shown in error."

"Did you say Mega Mantis is on the *loose*?" Lindsey stammered.

Walter nodded. "Dr. Leery is traveling in the hope that he might get the monster's coordinates and possibly tempt it to come to Riddle—or somewhere else."

I raised my hand. "Excuse me, but by any chance is this some kind of candid-camera reality show where my friend Garth is going to jump out from behind that curtain and yell 'GOTCHA'?"

Walter smiled. "No, Jesse. I'm afraid not."

"Why *us*?" Stella asked. "I mean, Oswald Leery has a huge number of fans. Why did he pick four random kids from Riddle to share his secret—and destroy the monsters?"

Walter cleared his throat. "That is a very good question, Stella. And I have a very good answer. No one was chosen randomly. You all have connections to the Bs. Jesse had his Uncle Rich "Danger" Ranger. Lindsey's grandfather Max took photos for the studio. And of course, Damon's family owns the old Drive-O-Rama."

"What about me?" Stella asked. "No one in my family even likes monsters, let alone B-Monsters with fourteen tentacles and death breath. Why am *I* here?"

Walter dimmed the lights and showed us a photograph up on the screen.

"Hey!" Stella said. "That's my Great Auntie San San. Where did you get that?"

"Your Great Aunt Sandra was one of the most popular B-Monster movie actresses *ever*. She won awards for all the roles she played. She was convincing as a spider lady or a gorilla tamer or a scientist from space. She was a mistress of disguise, the best of the Bs."

Stella got real quiet. "Great Auntie San San is an *actress*? She never leaves her house."

"Yes." Walter nodded. "But she went into hiding only *after* the B-Monsters started coming to life. She went a little, well . . . crazy."

"Crazy just like *you*, Stella!" Damon cried.

"Quit it, Molloy!" Lindsey yelled. "If this is going to work at all, we need to work together."

"I'm a little freaked out," Stella said. For the first time ever, she sounded unsure.

"Yeah? Well, I'm leaving," Damon said. He tried to wiggle out of his seat but he couldn't unlatch the buckle. I could understand why he wanted out of that place.

But, deep down, I kind of hoped this whole speech was the real deal. Helping Oswald Leery hunt down B-Monsters would be one hundred times cooler than making B-Monster movies of my own. We had to stay, no matter what. We had to help.

"Damon!" I said. "Remember the slime in Mr. Bunsen's classroom?"

"It's kind of hard to forget *that*," Damon said. "It smelled like *feet*."

"Don't you think we should investigate where that slime came from—and where our teacher went?" I asked pointedly.

"We're in the fifth grade, Jesse. We're kids, not monster exterminators."

Stella narrowed her eyes. "I'm getting ready to exterminate *you*, Damon."

"Can't we be *both* things?" I asked.

"I know it seems incredible," Walter added. "But you four really can help save the world from the B-Monsters."

"I can't even save my allowance," Lindsey cracked.

"Dr. Leery would never have enlisted your help if he didn't think you could do it. Everything goes back to the movies, and you four know them better than anyone," Walter said. "Now you have the resources and objects of the castle at your disposal, too."

I didn't know what to say. None of us did.

"Think it over," Walter said. "Go home and sleep on it. Take your time and see if you're ready to be the Monster Squad—or not."

It was very late by now. The sun had gone down. Walter offered us a ride in his limousine so we wouldn't have to take the bus back home alone. He pulled the car in the driveway and scurried back to lock up the castle.

The darkness gave me the creeps. The car's motor chugged. All around us were these enormous dark puddles. It must have poured rain while we were inside the castle watching Leery.

"Do you smell that?" I asked the others. There was that rotten stink again, the same one I'd smelled in our kitchen at home. I noticed a faint glow in the limousine's tinted windows.

"Oh, no!" I cried. "Get away from the car! Quick!"

We turned and ran behind some bushes. Before we could even count to ten, an enormous wave of slime shot straight up out of the limousine's moon roof—like a geyser.

"Get away from the car!" I wailed. "It's bigger than before!"

"That's sooo disgusting!" Lindsey said.

"I think I see teeth!" Damon said.

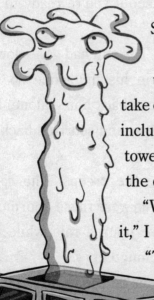

"Wait! Are those *ears*?" Stella asked aloud.

The green goo had risen up into the air and begun to take on several human qualities— including ears and arms! It towered over the limousine and the driveway.

"We have to make a run for it," I said.

"To the castle!" Stella said.

We rushed out from behind the bushes, but it was no use. The slime was so much bigger than all of us and it was blocking the way back inside. Damon started running away from the driveway. We followed him.

"Wait! Wait!" I said, stopping after a minute or so. "Where are we going? We have to face the B-Monster, not fear it!"

"Are you nuts?" Lindsey asked. "What do we face a tower of slime with, Jesse? Obviously it wants to eat us."

The slime gurgled loudly. It was growing even bigger in the darkness—and *man*, that thing was ugly. It looked hungry.

"This is bad," Lindsey said.

Slimo reached out for us with long, spindly, slimy fingers.

"Ruuuuuuun!" Damon cried. "While we still have the chance!"

"No, we can't run," Stella said, getting tough. "We have to fight."

The Ninja stood her ground. She assumed her karate positions in the dark. I could barely see her— or the slime. And then a bolt of lightning cracked and lit up the area where we stood.

"Aaaah!" we all screamed at the same time. Slimo was right here! We could really see it now, illuminated by the sudden flash of light.

Stella tried to intimidate the slime, but she had no power. An arm of slime extended as far as the eye could see.

"Look!" Damon said. "On the ground!"

I nearly keeled over when I saw what was there.

On the pavement between us and the limousine were two words, spelled out in slime:

STAY AWAY.

DO NOT TOUCH... OR ELSE

I spent the entire week thinking about the Bs—even more than usual, that is!

At school on Friday, I was tempted to rush right over to Lindsey, Stella, or Damon. But I didn't. We ignored one another and stuck to old friends. I think the idea of saving the world from Slimo had scared us all into silence.

At lunch, Garth kept bugging me about some dumb video game he wanted to play, but I wanted to talk about other stuff: Leery the director and Poe the crow, and of course, those slimy slime messages.

But I didn't say boo. We were the Monster Squad. It was all about big secrets now.

I tried to imagine what a Monster Squad uniform might look like. Puffy silver astronaut sleeves? Laser guns on holsters? Big fat goggles with triple-strength X-ray vision? Would Leery's special assignment be cool—or just terrifying?

After school, in the parking lot, I saw Stella sitting alone on a large rock. No big surprise there. I decided to break the silence.

"Hey," I said, walking toward her. "What's up?"

"You mean what's *down*, don't you?" Stella said. As she looked up, her long black hair fell right into her face. "Damon was right. We're doomed."

"No we're not," I said. "Quit being so negative."

"Every moment we hang out here, Slimo gets stronger," she said.

"I wish I knew what to do," I said. "I feel like he was just trying to scare us . . . or send us a warning . . . but why? What did it mean?"

Out of nowhere, Damon popped up. Today he was posse-free, but he kept checking behind him like he was being followed.

"Yo," Damon said. He squeezed in between Stella and me. "Hey."

"What's the matter with you?" I asked. "You look like a—"

"Shhhhh," Damon said.

I pointed to his T-shirt. "Did you wear that on purpose?"

Damon glanced down. His shirt read STAY AWAY!, just like Slimo's message from the day before.

"I'm keeping an eye out for Slimo," Damon said.

"Hey, you guys!" Lindsey called out. Her friends were nowhere to be seen. As she ran over to us, her camera flopped back and forth on her chest. "Did I miss anything?" She held up her camera. "Say slime!" she said.

"Funny, Lindsey," Stella said. "Is this really time for a photo op?"

"Why not? I think we should keep a record of things," Lindsey said, still snapping away. "If we're going to get Slimo or any of Leery's other B-Monsters, we need to get organized."

No one budged.

"Are we really going to do this?" I asked.

"Do what?" Damon asked back.

Lindsey gave him a knuckle-noogie. "Be the Monster Squad, dumbo!" she said.

Damon looked like he might knuckle-noogie her right back.

I stepped in.

"If we're going to do this," I said, "we need to do it right. We can't fight."

Stella grunted. "Fat chance. The fights are the best part."

I glared at her. "The Monster Squad is serious stuff. Stop goofing around."

"Okay," Stella said. "Then let's do it. *Seriously*. If we watch all the Bs again, we can figure out the best plan to eliminate Slimo."

Damon held up a bus schedule. "The bus for Leery Castle leaves in five minutes."

We grabbed our backpacks and headed for the stop. I didn't know what to think—or say. In the past twenty-four hours we'd gone from ordinary fifth-graders to freak fighters. I never thought I'd be a part of any organized club, let alone an entire Monster Squad.

Now we were heading back to the source of all the trouble, Leery Castle.

The ride up was quick, but the castle property seemed awfully quiet. We walked through the Crabzilla gates half-expecting a flapping Poe to fly out and greet us. But no one greeted us. The front door to the castle was ajar.

"Walter!" I called out. There was no answer, but we headed in anyway.

Daylight shined through the castle's stained-glass windows and gave everything inside the castle a purple or yellow hue. Each room in Leery Castle was stranger than the next, with trapdoors and suspended furniture and all sorts of buttons and switches marked DO NOT TOUCH . . . OR ELSE.

A sign like that only made me want to touch *everything*, of course.

"Walter!" Stella called up a flight of stairs.

No answer.

I moved into the round room and searched for the panel that released the secret slide down to the screening room. But nothing seemed to work.

We wouldn't be getting to the screening room via a slippery slide today. Instead, we hunted for a staircase to the basement level.

Once we actually got downstairs, it took Lindsey only a moment to find the door that read SCREENING ROOM. A door next to it read VAULT. We decided to head into the vault first to get the movies we needed to see.

I don't know what I was expecting to see, but it wasn't what we found. The vault was a black room with no windows. None! Shelves overflowed with reels and videos. DVDs lined the walls. I thought I knew Leery's movie collection, but there was so much here that I'd never even heard of or read about. Plus, this room had not been touched in a very long time. Everything was a dusty, grimy mess and nothing was alphabetical. We couldn't really tell if the tapes or reels were copies or real. I assumed Leery would have destroyed originals a long time ago.

I walked over to what should have been the *Slimo* section and saw three movies there that started with the letter *S*: *Snake Boy*, *Saved by the Beast*, and *Son of Slimo*. Luckily, it didn't take too long to find two other *Slimo* flicks we needed: *Slimo* and *Curse of Slimo* were buried in another pile across the room.

We carried *Slimo* and its two sequels into the screening room.

"Here goes nothing," I said. Stella hit PLAY on the projection machine.

As drops of slime appeared at the edges of the screen, I could practically smell the goo.

CURSES!
SLIMO AGAIN!

The B-Monster Vision used to film *Slimo* gives it one of the best special-effects scenes in all of Leery's movies. Just when you think the monster has drowned or disappeared, it rises from the swamp, ready to attack.

The ending with the exploding gas bubble gets me every time. I've never watched another movie where I felt like the screen was splurting at me. I love the fact that Slimo escapes without being destroyed in the first movie. That way, we still don't know what—if anything—is capable of killing the goo.

I took out a pencil and my small notebook, like all the best detectives do. If I was going to be a Monster Squad member, I needed to get serious about asking all the right questions.

Where does Slimo come from? Don't know.

Who does Slimo eat? Anyone and everyone—except for shoes.

Does Slimo really die in the first movie? No!!!

We popped in *Slimo*'s first sequel and waited for it to start.

In *Curse of Slimo*, the B-Monster shows up just before a cruise ship leaves port.

The action starts with a group of guests on a cruise ship. They are eating breakfast. Everything is perfect: the sun, the water, and the sky. Then breakfast arrives in oversize serving trays. Only it isn't breakfast at all. It is Slimo, disguised as breakfast! It oozes all over the rooms, swallowing cruise passengers (and whatever else it could eat, like pool chairs, inflatable rafts, and shuffleboard sticks) in great big gross gulps. Of course, it leaves a lot of sandals and flip-flops and a foul, foul stench behind in the process.

Damon loved this sequel the best. He was laughing so hard the whole time, I thought he was going to explode. Every time Slimo gulped down another object, Damon burped like a foghorn. At the end of the movie, it looks like Slimo drowns when it falls off the cruise ship during a bad lightning storm. Damon almost fell out of his chair.

Stella, of course, wasn't laughing one bit. She wanted to debate about how and why the slime dies— or *if* it dies at all in the sequel. After all, it hadn't died in the first flick. We couldn't agree. Lindsey thought it swam away. Damon and Stella both thought a deep-sea creature swallowed it. Maybe it just drowned?

If we didn't know for sure how Slimo died in the movies, how could we ever really figure out how to get rid of the monster?

I had to keep taking notes! There were answers here, on-screen. I just had to look closer.

The next sequel was called *Son of Slimo*. As that reel started up, heavy, dark music played in the background. This Slimo leaves trails of sludge everywhere like an enormous snail, even though it is the dead of winter.

In one of the scenes, Stella spotted a waitress at a restaurant scene. Was that Auntie San San? Walter had told us that Sandy appeared in almost every single B-Monster movie. We had to keep our eyes open!

By the end of the movie, after ingesting a dozen woodland creatures and the town sheriff, the winter

111

slime crawls onto a major highway during a major blizzard. It travels slowly for miles on the road until it finally just collapses. Or does it freeze? Or does it stop breathing?

"It's not dead!" Damon yelled as the movie ended. "Oswald Leery is tricking us!"

"Wait, I think he's just giving us clues," Stella declared. "In every movie we've watched, *water* is always around when the B-Monster gets destroyed. Maybe that's the answer to all our questions."

Was Stella right?

Slimo vanishes in water in the first movie. Then, in the first sequel, the ocean gets him again! But what about the last movie? In *Son of Slimo*, was it the blizzard—the *snow*—that kills the B-Monster? Snow is just frozen water, after all.

"You're probably right about the water," I said to Stella. "Except for the fact that if water kills the B-Monster, then how did it survive in our kitchen and bathroom sinks?"

Stella shrugged. "Oh, good point. This is so hard to figure out!"

"Maybe something is *in* the water," Lindsey said. "Like flesh-eating microorganisms."

"Are you kidding?" Damon said, making a face. "That's disgusting."

"No more disgusting than *you*," Stella said.

"You guys!" I cried. "We have to figure this out together."

All of a sudden, the lights went up in the projection room. I squinted at the light.

"Hello, Monster Squad," Walter said with his ominous voice.

I worried that he might be angry with us. After all, we'd come into the castle unannounced.

But he wasn't angry. He wanted to help.

"Found anything out about the real Slimo?" Walter asked.

Stella flipped her long black hair and sighed. "No, we're stuck. How does Slimo really die?"

"We know it has something to do with water," I explained. "But we don't know why."

"Isn't there something else you can tell us?" Lindsey asked.

"Perhaps," said Walter. "Perhaps there is something *in* the water that helps to destroy Slimo?"

"That's what I was thinking!" Damon cried.

I glared at Damon. He was taking credit for Lindsey's good idea.

"Okay, you guys, it's getting late," Stella said, looking annoyed. "I have to go home now and do my real homework. Sorry."

"How can you think about homework at a *slime* like this?" Lindsey cracked.

We all groaned loudly. Stella made a face.

"Have you visited some of the places where you saw the slime?" Walter asked. "Maybe that will help. That's what Dr. Leery always does."

"You're right!" Stella's face lit up again. "We can check out Mr. Bunsen's classroom tomorrow!"

"Good idea," Lindsey said.

"How are we ever going to get into school?" I asked. "Tomorrow is Saturday."

"I know a way in!" Damon said.

"You do?" I said.

"I'm not a member of the Monster Squad for nothing!" Damon said.

I smiled. We really were all in this together now! In order to get Slimo, all we had to do was get back to the scenes of the slime.

CHAPTER 14

WELCOME TO MOLDY CITY

Damon may be the fifth grade's most annoying bully, but he is also a total genius.

We sneaked into school the next day, Saturday, through the downstairs double doors. The basketball team played there on Saturday, but Damon figured that even though most basketball players and fans would not use the lower level, the doors would still be open.

He was right.

Damon also figured that Security Guard Spiker might be at the school building.

He was right about that, too.

But Spiker didn't keep us out. He said, "Howdy kids. Enjoy the game."

I think he knew we weren't there to play ball, but he let us in just the same.

When we sneaked up the stairwell to the third floor, however, we started to get nervous. The school was super-creepy when classes were out of session.

Mr. Bunsen's class was still blocked off with yellow police tape. We had to climb underneath to get inside the doorway.

The first thing that we noticed was the smell.

Everywhere we looked, it reeked, worse than ever.

"Maybe Slimo is already dead?" Lindsey suggested. "That would make life easier, wouldn't it?"

"Right," Damon said. "Like this going to be easy? I don't think so."

"Do you think this first Monster Squad mission is some kind of test?" Stella asked as she walked to the other side of the room.

"I feel like everything in life is a test," I mumbled. "And I'm *this close* to failing."

"Peeuuuw! All the leftover goop in here smells so bad," Lindsey said, fanning her nose. "I think I might—"

"Don't say it!" Damon cried. He pinched his nose hard and went into Mr. Bunsen's science closet. This place was usually off-limits. It was where Mr. Bunsen stored jars and specimens. He had a long shelf stacked with videocassettes and piles of papers, plus a slop sink and a refrigerator.

Lindsey and I followed Damon into the closet. Stella was still across the room.

"Hey, the fridge in here is open!" Damon cried as we turned the corner and saw the light glowing.

"And I guess we've found the source of the bad smell," I moaned, pinching my nose.

We spotted the problem right away. It wasn't slime, though. It was moldy cheese. There were dishes turning black, blue, and green with fuzz.

"How gross is *this*?" Lindsey said. "Welcome to Moldy City!"

"Is there anything grosser than old cheese?" Damon said.

"You mean besides your breath?" I joked.

"I'll pound you later for that," Damon groaned.

"Wait!" Lindsey said, peering deeper into the fridge. "Look!"

In the back, *way* in the back, was a row of test-tube vials in a small stand. Inside the vials was something green. It appeared to be glowing.

Slimo!

"Get one of those out."

Lindsey reached in and got it.

"Cool," Damon said. "This doesn't jiggle like the slime I saw in my bathroom."

"Let me see," I said, reaching for one of the vials. Damon was right. It didn't seem gooey at all. "But it has to be the same stuff," I said.

"So Mr. Bunsen can see Slimo, too . . ." Lindsey said.

"Just like we can," Damon added.

"What if one of these broke or fell and the slime poured out?" I suggested.

"Massive slimage!" Damon said.

Sluuuuurp.

We all turned our heads. It was coming from the classroom!

"Help!" Stella screamed.

We rushed out. Stella was standing on top of Mr. Bunsen's desk. On the floor, all around her was a green slime pool, quivering.

"Heeeellllp!" she cried again. She had assumed her best karate pose, but we already knew even the strongest kung-fu chop could not defeat this goo.

I panicked.

Without thinking, I started hurling things at the slime. First, I threw a vial from the fridge (because it happened to be in my hand). Then I reached for a binder from the classroom bookshelf. Damon started throwing, too. He pelted the slime with a few books. Lindsey joined in.

"What are you guys *doing*?" Stella screeched. "The slime is getting ready to eat me—not read to me!"

"If we feed it other stuff, maybe it'll be less hungry for you," Damon said.

Stella howled. The slime stretched up all the way to the ceiling, arching over her like a tidal wave of goo. It looked ready to swallow her in one hungry gulp! I could see hollow holes where its eyes belonged. It had teeth and arms!

Stella was in big trouble.

If she had been the main character in one of Oswald Leery's movies, this would have been the part where I yelled out, "Oh, nooooo! She's a goner!"

But I didn't yell that. This was Stella Min and she wasn't a goner. She was tougher than any of us! I had to help her.

I leaped onto another lab table and waved my arms around, trying to distract the slime. At first I wasn't sure the enormous blob could even see me. But slowly, it began to slime in a different direction, toward *me*.

"Damon! Lindsey! Help me! We can convince the slime to go in an opposite direction, like out the window," I said.

"Out the window?" Stella yelled at me. "So Slimo can destroy the rest of Riddle? That's exactly what Dr. Leery wants us to stop it from doing, Jesse! Bad idea!"

"Ooops," I gulped. "So what am I supposed to do?"

Damon let out a yelp. He was caught in the slime's

grip. One long Slimo arm had wrapped itself around Damon's ankle . . .

Sluuuuurp.

"Noooo!" Damon wailed. Within five seconds, he was half-covered in the stuff. "My legs!"

Sluuuuurp.

"What are we supposed to do now?" I shrieked. My thoughts raced. Damon was the meanest bully in the entire school and something seemed so right about him getting swallowed by a B-Monster, but I had to stop it.

"Lindsey!" I cried.

"Water!" she yelled, rushing back over to me. She had a pail in her hands. It was filled to the brim.

"Yes!" I cried as she raised it up.

Before she let go, however, I heard a sucking noise like the world's loudest straw slurp.

"Nooooo!" Stella cried.

But I couldn't see her.

"Oh, no!" Damon cried out. "Nooooo!"

We glanced over to Mr. Bunsen's desk, just in time to see the top of Stella's head disappear under a blanket of slime. She was gone—except for her pair of black shoes.

Damon looked ready to cry. His face went white. *He* was next.

Lindsey lifted the pail into the air. "Here goes nothing!" she cried, tossing the water over our heads.

"Sayonara, Slimo!" I screamed.

And we held our breath, waiting to see what would happen next.

THWUNK

I expected some kind of brilliant flash of light. Or a loud sucking noise. Anything that would show me the slime was on its way out.

Instead, the slime quivered and moved forward. It was even stronger than before!

"Oh, no! It's not working!" Damon yelled. "Ranger, I'm gonna get you for—"

Before he could finish his thought, the slime gulped him down whole.

I looked away. Things were not working out like we'd hoped. We were down to half a Monster Squad.

In the past two minutes, Slimo had gotten *stronger*.

My mind raced. Time was running out. If Lindsey and I got swallowed up, then there would be no one left to fight the B-Monster.

I tried to remember the *Slimo* movie facts.

"Jesse!" Lindsey said. "The slime is on *my* shoe now. Hurry!"

Slimo had twisted a tendril of slime up Lindsey's leg. It would come after me next.

I had to think faster.

In the first movie, Slimo slips away unharmed. But in the second movie, Slimo dies. He sinks into the water. But what is special about that water? Fish? Seaweed? Wait! It was the ocean. It was salt water. Salt? In the third movie, he was killed on a highway covered with snow. But what else was on the road? Wait! Salt! Road salt!

"I think I know what to do!" I blurted. "I just hope we have time—"

I darted back into the science closet, leaping over puddles of the green goo and sidestepping those long arms of slime that were trying so hard to grab me. This was trickier than the fifth-grade obstacle course! I'd never seen so much hungry slime in my whole life.

"Yes!" I said when I saw what I was looking for. I grabbed a huge canister from a shelf and raced back into the classroom. "Okay, Slimo! Get ready to DIE—for real!"

Thwunk.

I fell and skidded across the floor. Running into the classroom, I'd tripped on my own shoelaces—again. The canister in my hand opened up and released white dust all over everything.

Lindsey looked horrified. "What is *that*?" she asked.

I gasped as slowly, on contact, the slime slid off her legs and then her torso. It started to shrivel. My solution was working! Lindsey was free!

"Jesse!" Lindsey cried. "How did you do that?"

The canister was next to me on the floor. I held it up. On the side was one word: SALT.

"You figured it out," I told

Lindsey. "You were right when you said the answer was probably something *inside* the water."

There had been salt in the ocean water in *Slimo* and *Curse of Slimo*. And there was road salt during the blizzard in *Son of Slimo*.

"Thanks," Lindsey said. "Thanks for figuring it all out."

"Look!" I cried. The slime was shrinking.

"It's turning into some kind of green fog," Lindsey said.

Across the room, I heard groans.

Damon! Stella!

They were both barefoot, but they were back.

"Aaarrgh!" Stella moaned. "My head!"

"What happened?" Damon whimpered. "I feel like something my cat threw up. What is that smell?" He sniffed his shirt experimentally. "Oh, no, it's ME!"

"Jesse saved us!" Lindsey announced.

I looked over at Stella. She smiled.

It was the first time I remembered seeing her do that.

The green fog filled the room as the slime evaporated. Then a small voice came from the other side of the room.

"Hello?" a voice groaned.

I saw the figure step out of the fog like the Thermominator, a superhuman, temperature-controlled robot from another one of Leery's Bs.

But this was no B-Monster. This was Mr. Bunsen!

"Where am I?" Mr. Bunsen asked, running his fingers through a mass of sticky hair on his head. "Who are you kids?"

"Your students," Lindsey said matter-of-factly.

"Are you feeling all right?" I asked. He looked perfectly normal for someone who'd been swallowed up by goo for the past week.

"Where am I?" Mr. Bunsen repeated. "What is that smell? Did something die in here?"

I wanted to tell him the truth about what had happened. But I couldn't. At least not right away.

"There was a . . . gas leak . . ." I stammered.

"Yeah!" Stella chimed in. "You passed out. We saw you behind the desk and called the police and . . ."

"Why does my head feel like an elephant stepped on it?" Mr. Bunsen asked. "Is this some kind of prank?"

"I think maybe you should see a doctor," Lindsey said.

Mr. Bunsen stared at Stella's hand. She was holding one of the Slimo vials we'd taken from the refrigerator.

"Where did you get that?" Mr. Bunsen asked.

"We found these green vials

in the refrigerator. Why were you storing slime?"

Mr. Bunsen rubbed his head. "I don't remember," he said thoughtfully. "No, wait. It was last week. I saw something green and glowing come up from one of the manhole covers on the street. Yes, that's it. I was curious, so I took a few scientific samples."

"You saw the slime, too?" Damon said. "Whoa."

"So now we know Slimo does travel in the sewers!" Lindsey said. "If Mr. Bunsen saw it in the street like that . . ."

"And that's why Slimo came into our houses through the sinks and bathrooms," Stella said.

"Hold on. Did you say *Slimo*?" Mr. Bunsen asked.

Aha! He knew who Slimo was! It was time to admit the truth. If Mr. Bunsen had seen the slime in the street, then somehow he must have a connection to Oswald Leery just like us.

"Mr. Bunsen, I think we have something very important to tell—" I started to say, but he interrupted.

"Excuse me, can you please tell me where everyone is?" Mr. Bunsen moaned. "Do we have class now?"

"Yo, Mr. B, it's Saturday," Damon said. "No school today."

"Saturday?" Mr. Bunsen said. "But that can't be true. I just finished up my Wednesday morning prep work." He leaned against the large wooden chair near his desk and scratched his head. "This is most unusual," Mr. Bunsen said.

"Mr. Bunsen, do you know the real Oswald Leery?"

I asked, sounding a little like one of those reporters who grill people on TV news shows.

"You mean Leery the B-Monster movie director who lives up on the mountain?" Mr. Bunsen said. "As a matter of fact . . . Wait! Of course I do! I was going to see Leery just this week."

"You were?" Lindsey asked.

"Yes, Dr. Leery was at the library for a screening. I went to show him my slime samples, but it was too crowded and the librarian said it was kids only, so . . ."

"I saw you there," I admitted.

"You did?" Stella looked at me sideways.

I just shrugged. "I didn't think it meant anything at the time. I recognized your sneakers. The ones under that desk over there."

"Ahh," Mr. Bunsen chuckled. "I was wondering where those went."

"So what else do you remember?" Stella asked.

"I remember *everything* now!" Mr. Bunsen announced to us. "I remember the story my grandmother told me when I was a boy. She was a makeup artist on some of those old Leery movies. She has a collection of all the films in her room at

Riddle Retirement Village. *Slimo* was my favorite one. I've seen it dozens of times. In fact, we had just watched it together before I found the slime in the street . . ."

"*Before* you saw the slime?" I asked. "Are you sure?"

"Sure as I can be . . . with this monster headache," Mr. Bunsen said.

"*Monster* headache!" Damon blurted. He laughed aloud. "You said that right."

"Excuse me?" Mr. Bunsen interjected.

Before I could convince Damon to shut up, he blabbed the whole truth.

"Mr. B, it was a giant slick of slime that ate you," Damon said. "Not some gas leak. It was Slimo. And after you, it ate me and Stella, too. Dude, it was *gross*."

"It *ate* me?" Mr. Bunsen looked woozy. "I think I should sit down now," he said.

"Don't worry," I explained, cutting in. "We saved you. The slime is gone for now. But it will come back unless we destroy the original *Slimo* movie. We can explain more later. You have to believe us."

"I'm not sure what I believe right now," Mr.

Bunsen said, his voice trailing off. He looked shaken up.

"I bet the original *Slimo* is still at the library!" Damon said.

"The library closes at five," Stella chimed in. "It's four o'clock now. We'd better go."

"I think I may call that doctor," Mr. Bunsen said.

"We can explain everything later, I promise!" I said as we raced out of the classroom.

"Very well," Mr. Bunsen cried. "Good luck."

As we headed downstairs, I felt a little worried about Mr. Bunsen. But I also felt a huge sense of relief.

Slimo was gone.

At last, things would have to get real.

I just hoped that Ms. Shenanigans would be willing to hand over the original movie reel—before Slimo came back.

A SIZZLE IN THE AIR

"All we have to do is go back in, grab the reel, and go," said Stella as we climbed the steps to the library.

Unfortunately, it wasn't quite that simple. There was a lecture that afternoon, so the library was crowded. Ms. Shenanigans sent us into her office to wait.

We sat there for a while until Stella got the bright idea to start snooping. Frantically, we searched the shelves.

"Do you see it anywhere?" I asked.

We searched high and low. Damon found a copy of *Son of Slimo*, but it wasn't the original reel, and it was too damaged to watch. Then Lindsey discovered a crate marked MOVIES under Ms. Shenanigans's desk. There was a reel case marked ORIGINAL COPY with the word *SLIMO* in red ink. What a relief!

I lifted it out to get the reel, but I got the surprise of a lifetime.

There was no reel inside! There was a videocassette instead. The library had shown a video when we saw *Slimo*, not a reel.

"Oh no," Damon sighed. "We made a big mistake. This isn't the original movie! It isn't here!"

"Wait!" I said. "Remember what Mr. Bunsen told us? He watched *Slimo* with his grandmother *before* we all saw it at the library. And then Mr. Bunsen saw the slime on Monday. We didn't watch *Slimo* here until Tuesday."

"What if his grandmother is the one with the original copy?" Stella asked.

"To the Riddle Retirement Village!" Lindsey cried.

We rushed out and thanked Ms. Shenanigans. The retirement village was within walking distance, but we had to hurry. We couldn't risk the chance that Mrs. Bunsen or anyone there might screen the movie and release the B-Monster again!

When we arrived, Mrs. Bunsen was sitting in the guest room with another visitor. I recognized the hair from behind! It was Mr. Bunsen!

He held out his hand to me. In it was a reel. I looked

close. It was the original reel of *Slimo*. He handed it to me.

"After you left, I started thinking about what you were saying," he said. "When my head finally stopped throbbing . . . I rushed over here."

I took the reel in my hands. "I can't give this back to you," I told Mrs. Bunsen.

Mrs. Bunsen nodded. "That's fine, dearie," she said with a wink. "I have a copy on DVD, too. My grandson is always borrowing my reels and making copies."

"Other reels?" I asked. I made a note. I needed to talk to Mr. Bunsen about that another time. For now, the most important thing we had to do was take *Slimo* out of this place and destroy it once and for all.

After we left the retirement home, however, I wasn't sure how. I clutched the reel in my hand. I couldn't believe that *this* had unleashed enough slime to suck up the entire town.

"What are you waiting for?" Stella asked me.

We all stopped short on the sidewalk.

"Let's just do it now," Damon said.

I held out the reel and we each took turns pulling

the film off like dental floss. We pulled and pulled until there was nothing left to pull. Then we tore it to bits.

Lindsey dumped it into a trash can and we all headed for home.

On the way, a familiar limousine pulled up next to us. Walter rolled down his tinted window.

"Climb in," he said.

We piled into the limo. Stella was all ready to spill the beans about our afternoon. We had a lot to tell Walter about *Slimo*.

But he already knew.

He congratulated us on getting the B in record time.

"Dr. Leery owes you his thanks," Walter said. "He's on his way back from Malaysia right now."

"Did he find Mega Mantis?" asked Damon.

"Not yet." Walter shook his head. "But he's getting closer. And Dr. Leery still owes you that personal tour of Leery Castle."

"I can't wait," Lindsey said.

"How did you know we'd defeated Slimo and destroyed the reel?" I asked. "When you pulled up in the car, how did you know what had happened?"

Walter smirked. "No magic tricks," he admitted.

"Dr. Leery got a call from Mr. Bunsen. He told him that the four of you had saved his life. He said that he was getting the original reel for you."

"Wow," I said. "Mr. Bunsen said all that?"

Walter nodded. "In honor of your recent accomplishments, Dr. Leery and I wanted to present you all with tokens to commemorate your first successful mission as the Monster Squad. After all, this is only the first of many adventures for you all."

I gulped. That sounded so exciting and terrifying all at the same time. But Stella was a little more gung-ho.

"Bring on the Bs!" she said, assuming the best karate pose she could while still sitting in the limousine seat.

"Yes," Walter said. "The next ones will be here soon enough. In the meantime, I have a few tokens of appreciation for you from Dr. Leery and me."

"Wow," I said, eyeing a bag on the seat next to him. "I sure do love surprises!"

"Me too," said Lindsey.

"First gift!" Walter said. "Goes to Damon Molloy."

Damon took his small box and ripped off the silver paper.

"No way! Cool!" Damon cried when he saw what was inside. It was a paperweight, shaped like a blob with an arm sticking out.

"Hey," Lindsey joked. "That looks like Mr. Bunsen, before he came back to school and after Slimo ate him!"

"Or ate *me*!" Damon smirked.

We laughed.

Next, Walter handed a package to Stella.

It was a signed book. She read the title aloud: *Woman of 1,000 Faces: Sandra Lee, Queen B* by A. Gal. Inside were photos of Stella's Great Auntie San San. She looked different in every photograph. In some she was dressed like a monster and in others she looked like a princess. She really had been the mistress of disguise.

"Wow," Stella said. "Who knew?"

"Lindsey, here is something special for you, too," Walter said. He handed her a teeny box.

"What could this be?" Lindsey said as she lifted off the top. Inside was a beautiful necklace with a charm on it: a drop of green slime.

"*Hold on*," Lindsey said. "If I drop this, it won't suddenly come to life and eat my cat, will it? Because the last thing in the world I would ever want to deal with is—"

"No, Lindsey," Walter interrupted. "It's not actual Slimo residue. Just resin."

I hoped Walter was saving the best prize—*my prize*—for last. I'd told him all about Dad's collections of cards and posters and old issues of *B-Monster Galaxy* magazines. I hoped he'd give me some one-of-a-kind something to add to the pile.

"What about Jesse?" Damon asked Walter. "He's, like, our fearless leader."

"Ah, yes. Jesse. You *are* fearless, as it turns out. Good for you."

Walter reached into his pocket and produced a small flat box. He handed it to me with a smile. *What is it?* I wondered. Was it a book? It would have to be very small to be a book.

I ripped off some green slime-colored tissue paper and opened the edge of the box.

When I saw what was inside, I nearly passed out.

It was an original *Slimo* collectible card—the one I'd wanted so much—one of five existing *Slimo* cards in the whole entire universe!

"Where did you get this?" I screamed.

"Oswald Leery has ways of making dreams come true. I hope it's what you wanted."

"You know it is! Thank you!"

Walter reached out and squeezed my shoulder. "Thank *you*," he said.

I knew that the card was valuable and that I should have put it somewhere for safekeeping right away,

but I stuck it in my pocket instead. I wanted to have it pressed close to me right now. I wanted to savor the moment.

The limousine stopped at Riddle Park and we all got out and went for a stroll together.

Lindsey was all excited about taking a photograph of us in celebration of our first B-Monster adventure. She set her timer and put the camera up on a bench to take the photograph. We posed with our gifts.

As the camera flash went off, I felt a sizzle in the air. Sometimes it's like that around Riddle. The weather gets wild or weird. You can almost feel the buzzing in our ears.

Then I felt something else—on my shoulder.

When I looked, I saw Poe, the crow.

"Hello, bird," I cawed.

Poe opened his beak and let out a squawk, like he was telling me something important.

Everyone else on the Monster Squad laughed, even Stella.

And in that moment, I knew that nothing about my life in Riddle would ever, *ever* be the same.